BETWEEN THE DEVIL AND THE DUSK

PATRICK IRELAND

The Book Guild Ltd

First published in Great Britain in 2024 by
The Book Guild Ltd
Unit E2 Airfield Business Park,
Harrison Road, Market Harborough,
Leicestershire. LE16 7UL
Tel: 0116 2792299
www.bookguild.co.uk
Email: info@bookguild.co.uk
X: @bookguild

Copyright © 2024 Patrick Ireland

The right of Patrick Ireland to be identified as the author of this
work has been asserted by them in accordance with the
Copyright, Design and Patents Act 1988.

All rights reserved. No part of this publication may be
reproduced, transmitted, or stored in a retrieval system, in any form or by any means,
without permission in writing from the publisher, nor be otherwise circulated in
any form of binding or cover other than that in which it is published and without
a similar condition being imposed on the subsequent purchaser.

This work is entirely fictitious and bears no resemblance to any persons living or dead.

Typeset in 10.5pt Adobe Garamond Pro

Printed on FSC accredited paper
Printed and bound in Great Britain by 4edge Limited

ISBN 978 1835740 033

British Library Cataloguing in Publication Data.
A catalogue record for this book is available from the British Library.

"Some people are always dreaming of travel and adventure in order to give themselves airs and an aura of heroism in other people's eyes. Then, when they find themselves in the middle of an adventure and in peril, they begin to think, 'What a fool I was. Why on earth did I put myself in this position?'."

The Iron King by Maurice Druon

Part One

Chapter One

I had, of course, wanted to be based in Tokyo, where loud neon lights can fry your retina from a casual glance and pounding sound rays can blind your ears upon impact. Before submerging into the city's foreign fuzz, your senses are totally masked in this unique ambience. Tokyo is the most densely packed place on the planet – a city so vast its metropolitan population of 38 million is over a dozen times greater than some nations. A city with its own concrete consciousness where ideas and identity appear to be tripping to infinity. Yes – Tokyo is a unique speck from the other billions of settlements on the hurtling rock we all call home.

The July rain violently rattled the plane delivering me to Tokyo. Its turbulence on our descent shook us like ragdolls so completely that, for a moment, I thought the terrible convulsions would rip apart and disassemble the craft in mid-air. My jet-lagged mind could almost imagine the small round windows slipping from their rubber sheaths, the fuselage following momentarily afterwards, the floor falling away as the plane broke up, and my seatbelt gracefully uncoupling as I plummeted into oblivion.

The landing bell pulled me back to reality with a clang. I peered out the rain-clotted windows framing an endless glow from a sea of shimmering kaleidoscopic rainbows. Soon our steep descent brought the rapidly approaching cityscape into view. I braced myself for reanimation after the exhausting, almost twelve-hour flight into Haneda Tokyo International Airport.

Haneda is the main international artery into the heart of Japan. It is built on reclaimed land dragged from the sea depths over a span of six decades. Our plane circled over Tokyo Bay like the many other aluminium vultures readying to regurgitate their passengers from every corner of the globe in an unbroken cycle since US Commodore Matthew C. Perry and his Black Ships opened Japan to the West by gunpoint on 14 July 1853. The airport has three distinct terminals built over decades. Their individual styles range from a 1950s theme of austere Soviet-style concrete, to a 1980s refined and practical post-modern approach, to, finally, a terminal like a steel cathedral filled with shimmering, jittery glass. The latter was my plane's temporary home.

I was shell-shocked from jet lag and dehydrated by the flight's pure caffeine diet. After stumbling off the plane to an immigration booth, an agent scanned both index fingers and took my photograph for an instant check across dozens of global databases to confirm that I – Michael Brown – was not a known terrorist. Having passed the test, I propped myself up against a nearby pillar to wait for my luggage. Finally, luggage in hand, I entered the arrivals lounge and searched for a sign with my name on it. And there it was – a Japan Exchange and Teaching Programme (otherwise known as JET) company sponsor held one up with my name on it. I connected with him and was then hurriedly daisy-chained from one JET volunteer to the next across the terminal. It felt like we were out-of-place refugees dancing a mis-stepped waltz. Dozens of top eateries along the terminal edges called out to my empty stomach like sirens. But there was no time for that. Like toddlers, the JET company sponsor briskly chaperoned us out of the terminal and onto a bus bound for Tokyo. Settled on the bus, I glanced around. Some of my soon-to-be classmates acted like a kinetic bundle of nerves edging on mini breakdowns. Others simply dozed during the final one-hour journey to Tokyo. I joined my dozing companions.

When I came to and looked out the window, the Tokyo night was a blaze: a whirl of people and video screens. The city seemed to thrash to its own beat. It was lit up so brightly it almost denied the night's hard-won throne. Each street was a canvas of crowded faces. An infinite number of skyscrapers assaulted the heavens and flanked us as we pulled up to Keio Plaza Hotel – a man-made giant with polished brass doors glinting like gold and a white-gloved doorman who ushered us in as gracefully as a ballerina. Like a herd of wrung-out Vandals, we dragged ourselves in with weak abandonment.

In my five-star hotel room, I began to regain my composure and organised my basic facilities to prepare for the first day of the JET programme's three-day teaching assistant orientation the next morning. I ignored the no doubt helpful 300-page manual at the bottom of my bag. There was no way I could tackle that now. But after my second cigarette of the night, my daily routine, I had become too awake and hotwired on their cocktail of nicotine and adrenalin to contemplate sleeping. My two JET roommates seemed to have little interest in anything other than sleeping and had made it clear that my pacing-puffing presence was nothing more than a growing annoyance. So I decided to visit the bar for some liquid refreshment that, I hoped, would help me sleep later.

Chapter Two

The truth be known, I don't know why I decided to pursue the JET assistant English teacher programme. Perhaps my main goal had been to avoid "real" work and put off growing up for as long as practically possible. After frantic internet searches and hurried enquiries, I found no better way to do this then escaping to the other side of the globe on someone else's – in my case, the Japanese government's – dime.

I had applied for the job the previous October, five months ago. I was due to finish my master degree in English Literature the following July. As graduation grew closer, I sank into deep melancholy knowing I could no longer avoid real-life responsibilities and challenges. During this stressful time, I accidentally learnt about the JET programme after clicking on a cultural exchange internet link. When I discovered the programme could last for five years (if I was lucky), the offer became even more tempting. Anything to avoid returning home and spending my days dodging my father's disproving gaze and my mother's incessant preaching. In fact, my mother had been very suspicious of the programme. Before I left for Japan, she bluntly stated that a programme taking only three days to learn the basic tactics for teaching a foreign language to children sounded like a scam to her. She went on to point out that I had zero natural skills for languages, and the Japanese language structure was not even close to English. I had, she noted sharply, no knowledge of my host country's social code, which had customs the polar opposite to mine. I, of course, ignored her prescient warnings.

Chapter Three

I was glad I had the chance to go out for a night on the town in Tokyo before the shock and awe of the three-day teaching course commenced. I needed to unwind my nerves and kickstart my jet-lagged senses with loud bars and hard liquor and went down to the hotel bar. Disappointingly, the red-brick walls and matching leather chairs were occupied by Japanese businessmen and empty of westerners. A king's ransom in alcohol elixir gleamed like bottle-shaped ingots behind the bar. An immaculately suited barman served drinks from clear vodka to golden whiskey easily worth more than an average worker's yearly salary. I looked around and found only one other white man, unknown to me, sporting a JET programme t-shirt. I decided to introduce myself.

Johnny informed me halfway through a hard handshake that the rest of my temporary weekend family would soon be scattered to every corner of Japan's five-island archipelago. We noted how they were either currently immobile from jet lag or comatose from nerve-jolting culture shock. Either way, they just wanted to crawl into bed, hoping that the old proverb "it will seem better in the morning" would prove true.

Johnny was the one exception to our colleagues' temporary narcoleptic condition. Two, if I included myself. We were the only ones up for some nocturnal antics. I noted how the half-a-day flight had seemed like a mere roundtrip drive to the corner shop for this live wire. I felt that if he plugged his fingers into the nearest wall socket, his energy would easily light up Tokyo with enough spare energy for Japan's 125-million-person basic household needs. The lucky bastard wanted to go and see the big city instantly, despite the fact he was based there for the next year, less than an hour from our hotel. This was a man who obviously never spared a moment of life navel-gazing and could energise the least energetic of people in the blandest of circumstances.

So, mentally drained and physically unstable, we set out to get lost in the city's oriental wonders and sample its delights. For me, this meant basic drinking. For Johnny, any of the city's varieties of exotic flesh would do – and by the avalanche of innuendos he was dropping, that meant any girl or boy. The most severe warnings of our JET keepers regarded the hazards of getting stranded in the Russian roulette of Japanese public toilets running from ultra-modern self-cleaning to simple toilet paperless shitholes in the ground. This situation seemed comical next to the real chance of being sold into white slavery, something that occurs to this day in some parts of East Asia.

We had neither the urge nor ability to stray too far from the hotel. As the night neared 10:00p.m., the crowds increased, streaming with mostly oriental faces, an occasional Caucasian, and an ever-rarer face of the darker vintage. We finally arrived at the fabled red arches of Kabukichō – the largest red-light district in Asia (if not the whole world). They shimmered like a beacon of sin beckoning us onwards. We dodged and wove through the crowds. Many focused solely on their phones, having long before become numb to the novelty of the decadence and moral degradation of the place. Hawkers gave out flyers while calling out in sharp Japanese and broken English to entice passers-by into their lairs. Voluptuous manga girls with micro miniskirts and endlessly promising smiles stared down dead-eyed from fifty-foot billboards, coyly beckoning in silent gap-toothed titillation horror. Below, their blood-and-flesh sisters obliviously paraded the streets in the same sexy cloud as their billboard siblings. Hostess clubs lined the streets, the predators fluttering their eyes from professional posters. Here, people, both males and females, earn their living by offering paid companionship to those too busy and unable to connect with others in the real world. Instead, they pay for the illusion of enticements by companions with movie-star looks and promise-filled smiles. Signs blazed for every sex fetish from peep shows to bathhouses, their banners covering brick building walls like dense barnacles. Like kids in a candy store, Johnny and I eagerly walked through the rambunctious chaos. The ubiquitous smiles couldn't hide the misery of the perpetrators, second only to their prey. Everything was for our shallow amusement, making us the most guilty of parties. Ironically, a few streets uptown, local politicians campaigned passionately, besieging street corners to entice passers-by with fake truths and inflated promises like their contemporaries the world over. A companion piece to what we found inside the red arches of Kabukichō.

Finally, we turned into Golden Gai – the most famous drinking spot in the Shinjuku special ward. There was no lack of bars, but space was conspicuously rare. Many bars sat less than ten people, some accepting members or regulars only. Others only catered to privileged clientele like jazz enthusiasts or exploitation film connoisseurs. Everyone sat in ramshackle rows like dozens of tiny private enclaves in the world's greatest metropolis.

As there was no place or welcome for us, we pushed onto the main road where Western-franchised eateries lined both sides. They had the look of chain bars strung with metres of too-bright LED lights. Their plastic leather seats gave off an odorous smell and a continuously cracking sound as ass cheeks repositioned themselves. There was as much authenticity there as in fast-food restaurants the world over. Here, the people were mostly tourists made paranoid from jet-lag and too much sake. They had chosen the fast-food familiarity of this place for fear of losing their way if they dove deeper into the city. Besides these lost souls, huddles of off-duty workers from nearby hotels and shops congregated in groups, their uniforms dishevelled and politeness absent, avoiding home for any number of reasons.

We eventually found ourselves by neither want nor accident in a bar with a light mixture of Western decor and heavy Japanese beverages. The place was opposite the Hanazono Shrine – the Mecca where businessmen go to pray for success in the new year. Our lethargic flight limbs had finally reached the limits of reasonable walking distance from the hotel. The air was thick with a dozen foreign lingos, all as meaningless to us as they would be to monkeys. Air-conditioned wheeze left beer glasses clammy. Cigarette smoke (its nicotine scent brewed with dozens of ethnic fragrances), perspiration and hints of alcohol-laced desperation layered the atmosphere. The beer was dense and strong. We found a table and sat down, circling each other with fractured and strained conversation as we tried to find insights and exploitable weaknesses. Rain began streaking the windows next to our table. Looking out, we saw pedestrians quickly unsheathe their umbrellas and erect them like a choreographed dance in some well-rehearsed performance. Their umbrellas came in many styles and patterns. Some were sturdy black, others a mere practical extension for the weary businessman, a shield from life's mundane miseries. There were also small, impossibly cute, domed cartoon animal umbrellas, whose oddly shaped ears caught the rain and deflected it onto their owners just for giggles. As the rain increased, so did the fast-forward of cars and mopeds – car tires screeching and mopeds dodging the collage of people crossing the street before disappearing out of view to carry on with their lives. In the distance, we could hear the din of a politician canvassing support for the next election from his sound truck, its battery of speakers fighting nature's rage and, more importantly, general voter apathy. His efforts seemed to be naught due to living in a country so polite that the main political party has had no proper opposition for over half a century, such is Japan's society's general level of almost total conformity.

We sat there watching the outside scene while downing our drinks and verbally circumnavigating each other like boxers in a ring. The weariness of twelve hours' air travel followed by a dazed bus commute into Tokyo made the effect of the alcohol we were consuming rapid and heavy. Our slurred conversation was testament to that.

'Can you fucking believe it? The next year is going to be pretty much an all-expense-paid holiday in Tokyo, one of the world's largest playgrounds!' Johnny raved.

This was the sort of man who didn't try a lick to contain his excitement for debauchery while sober, so when half pissed, his hedonism was infinitely multiplied.

'Speak for yourself. I get shipped off down south to god knows where the day after tomorrow. Hell, I can't even pronounce the place yet, and it took me the best part of an hour to find the region on a map.'

'Is it a city, town or village?' His excitement having decreased.

'It's a small village called Haifuku Kawakami on a coastal river off-shoot. It's a suburb of the small historic city of Hagi.

There are a number of small islands and beautiful bays in the area. So in my spare time I can go scuba diving – the only bright spot in an ocean of dullness. Apart from that, there is nothing exceptional, while you get all this!'

I made a sweeping, arched motion with both hands. Johnny grinned a knowing reply like a poker player with a royal flush to a lousy hand of ace high.

'What year are you teaching, Johnny? I got kindergarten or nursery school kids, whatever nouns you Australians call your infants.'

'Middle school, eleven to fifteen. Can't say I am much bothered. I'll just pretend I'm talking down to my younger brother. He'll testify I'm an expert in the field.'

After a barrage of awkward laughter, jet-lag haze finally gripped us. We unsteadily but merrily sloped back to our hotel rooms, hoping not to disturb our respective roommates but drunk enough not to care if we did. They were the ones who had had the good sense to get a solid night's sleep as a foundation for tomorrow's lessons, as opposed to our bedrock of strong whiskey and weak water.

Chapter Four

I spent the night with my ears shaking from my roommates' snores and my head spinning from too much drink. When I finally fell asleep, too exhausted to care, it was shallow and restless. I snapped awake to the muffled shrill of what sounded like overly enthusiastic orgasmic screaming from the floor below. I sighed mournfully, knowing there would be no more sleep for me that day.

I looked around the still-dim room. The thick curtains covering the windows neither deafened the city's audible hum nor mellowed the flash of its bright lights sliding around them. Outside, skyscrapers cast claw shadows across the windows. From a small window opening, the curtains rippled as though from an animal's roar. For a small-town boy like me, the experience was fascinating while vaguely terrorising.

***

We had to wear a suit to the orientation days with large stick-on name badges prominently displayed. I barely managed to scrawl my name on the right side of legible due to hangover jitters. This fact had been drilled into our skulls – from the first interview to the previous night's quick meeting – as threateningly as a sergeant major's instructions to new whimpering privates. It could not be a white shirt and black tie combo affair because that is standard Japanese funeral attire, and it would be seen as a bad omen. Neither could we wear cartoon or novelty ties because that would be advertising our low-level self-esteem and high-level attention-seeking disorder, so I played it bland and safe with charcoal-grey jacket and pants and light navy shirt. When at last I groggily made my way to the Western-style breakfast buffet, the buffet was in its death thralls. It had been picked clean as efficiently as starving vultures strip their prey.

The first session started promptly at 9:00a.m. in the conference room. It continued in terrific boredom until 6:00p.m. with only a half-hour lunch break and a few ten-minute toilet breaks. Our chairs were nothing but cruel, like a minor medieval torture device where any posture apart from legs systematically straight and eyes bolted forward resulted at best in irritating cramps and at worst crippling back pain. The squeaking dry marker bleeding onto the white board sounded like a jack hammer pounding my hangover, amplified a thousand-fold by my almost sleepless night. We each sat at desks two feet apart, almost regimental in formation. It was as if this was our final-year examination, not a series of casual introductory lectures to help guide us for the next twelve months. We covered riveting topics such as basic currency facts and the different necessary insurance forms for the most minor activity and adventures. The morning session dragged on, and I was glad I could find the same lesson in the textbook for a hurried review later when my head was not so heavy and my wits sharper. Today, it was taking all my strength to win the war against sleep.

Lunchtime finally came. The humdrum canteen dashed any high expectations of refreshment. It was so sterile it's barely worth describing – think of a poor school's cafeteria totally drained of its little style. I sat with three other boring newbies I'd briefly met and forgotten the day before. I quickly scanned the room for Johnny, but he was nowhere to be seen. I found out later that he was in a different class because high school required distinct teaching techniques. After lunch, with barely enough time to digest our food, we were swiftly herded back to the monochrome chore of lessons. It was a subtle hint that, after all, this was a business and not a mere pleasure trip. I definitely had to question the logic of two full-day cram sessions less then twenty-four hours after arriving from a twelve-hour flight.

Thankfully, the next day I was not hungover and was one of the first to get to the breakfast buffet before it was picked clean by my fellow hyenas. Unfortunately, that was the only highlight of the day. Our morning session covered the tactics of teaching grammar. The grammar lessons were just another episode of blunt-force academia repeatedly slamming students with facts. I regurgitated them in sync with the rest of the class, like a chorus. The structure could not have been more counterproductive. I concluded that whether conceived by a sadomasochist or a fool, neither had ever been a lecturer or professional educator. The day droned on, rapidly killing any enthusiasm I might have had for my chosen vocation for the next year.

The afternoon's manners and etiquette sessions were worse. At least you could adlib the morning's grammar lessons and get away unnoticed by the bored teacher. Now the high-grade Japanese business etiquette trainers, at razor-sharp attention, were ready to pounce on a single mistake. I suspect they harboured a permanent scorn for us. The grind of their profession – having to evaluate a new gallery of fools every other day – had long vanquished any joy for work they may have had at one time. Determined to make us comply properly, they dragged us, one by one, to the front of the class to practise how to bow. We learnt that a degree too high or low was a crime almost on par with regicide. The tutorial on giving and receiving business cards was as serious and as theatrical as taking religious vows.

The lectures soon made it clear that ninety per cent of our vocation for the next year would be common sense, with little help from the ten per cent knowledge blitzkrieg of the last two days. The whole endeavour was really about having had the fortune to be born on the correct continent. Being an assistant English teacher would mostly boil down to being an extra pair of hands for marking and eyes for crowd control. My brain would be thoroughly underused for the next year. In my opinion, that was a definite plus.

Thankfully, the day was almost done. The final lesson was an overview of Japan's criminal law and how to report minor crimes and deal with police if approached. My apathetic brain didn't even attempt to clear that final hurdle. Overall, I felt I had learnt very little. The previous forty-eight hours felt like a flashback to my first days at university when my brain was often more sodden by drink than serenaded by lectures. That evening there was a sightseeing tour put on by the JET team, including an authentic Japanese meal at the end. Never being a man to pass a chance to be fed for free, I decided it was my duty to attend.

Chapter Five

The training was finally complete. I saw Johnny only once the next day when we passed in the hotel lobby less than an hour before my scheduled departure to my southern exile in Haifuku Kawakami. We quickly exchanged email addresses before he rushed to find his new home; he was expected that afternoon due to his placement's nearness. I said my farewells as sincerely and as graciously as I could to people I had known barely more than a weekend and would probably never see again. We were about to be scattered like dandelion seeds over the country, carried by the wind of anticipation to the 421 inhabited islands, some to take root and bloom, others to drift and fail.

I arrived at Tokyo's main train station, Shinjuku Station, a half-hour early. The station is the largest and busiest transport hub on the globe with no less than 3.5 million trips a day. After navigating its alleys and staircases, I eventually found my platform with fifteen minutes to spare. The bullet train arrived, floating on magnets as if pulled from the pages of a sci-fi novel. I boarded, and it set off at a shattering speed to take me to Haifuku Kawakami, a village in the Yamaguchi Prefecture. Just outside the ancient city of Hagi, this would be my home for the next year. My Japanese odyssey had finally begun and, like the maverick Odysseus 2,000 years before, I would soon find myself on a journey where my choices would be gambled by fate and luck rather than the year of stale teaching I had signed up for.

After pulling out of the station, the first thing I noticed, niggling my subconscious, was the silence. Absent was the standard rhythmic rattle of wheels almost ricocheting off their rails and the slapping symphony of a normal train's undercarriage on traditional lines. It was mildly disconcerting to watch the scenery glide by as the train accelerated without a whisper of friction or the slightest jolt. We reached the full speed of 200 miles per hour frighteningly fast. My carriage was only half filled. A few suited businessmen tapped on their laptops intently, never breaking to glance up from their work. A couple of families spoke in low tones, and few others sat in almost meditative silence.

Tokyo's grey concrete skyrise blocks skipped by endlessly. Never in my extensive travels have I known it to take so long to leave a place, which only added to the sense of its huge size. Slowly, as we passed the city's outskirts of dense housing blocks ribboned with tiny alleyways, the fields began filtering in. These finally morphed into small towns constricted by motorways until, finally, there was only the sea and the industrial powerhouse factories on the shore to the right and endless rice paddies on the left, punctuated by the odd village. In less than a decade, these villages would probably be consumed by the Tokyo behemoth already nibbling at their heels.

Only now did my mind drift back to the very beginning of my adventure, long before the excitement of arriving in the Land of the Rising Sun. On a weary November morning, I was slumped in my university student residence, my education in its twilight, its hourglass dribbling to the last few grains. I stared at the JET application form, mocking me with its blankness. My twenty-one years felt empty of any real-world knowledge, and I felt on the verge of almost frightened. In two hours, I had managed to write only my name, date of birth and address. The Statement of Purpose was causing a writer's block. I needed a positive overtone to shield my intention to use a government project to fund my true purpose of self-imposed exile, thus escaping any notion of real adult responsibility. That would hardly be endearing to the person assessing my application.

The internet was my salvation as it, too, has many other idlers and reprobates. I was the humble Moses, the laptop my private Mount Sinai, its endless knowledge my personal finger of god. I raided various websites, pillaging their ports for any scrap of useful information, a few lines to be copied, a couple of paragraphs to be reordered, to answer questions like: Why Japan? and Why JET? I exaggerated my work experience to elevate it from a simple barman to deputy manager. I fabricated my supposed passion for teaching to become something greater than an alien autopsy video and fairy's photo hoax combined. Then, I inflated my six-week Duke of Edinburgh bronze placement experience as a third-rate assistant to a six-month prime leadership role. To finish my masterpiece of misinformation, I told them about my deep interest in Japan and its culture as well as what I would contribute and hoped to receive in return. Seeing this was an all-or-nothing situation more than a paid, glorified, government-funded culture exchange, I kept my answers vague and broad, littering them with clichés such as "learning about other cultures" and "trading different experiences". My last ace in the hole to back up all my bluffs – my master's degree in English Literature. I was yanked out of my reverie by the passenger beside me trying to climb over my knees.

Stepping off the train at Shin-Yamaguchi Station, I first noticed how small the station was, considerably less busy compared to Tokyo's Shinjuku Station. The station was utterly lifeless; it could be in any backwater grove around the globe. The few people there disembarked and dispersed instantly into the humdrum rhythm that only locals possess. I headed towards a single set of stairs and started the ascent to ground level. My legs were lightly cramped from 4.5 hours of sitting, my back slightly stiff – inflictions of travel idleness. The station was a long, white, rectangular box as bland and soulless as could be imagined, rescued by a vertical garden meandering through the centre. A flush of vibrant green suspended from the ceiling and, canvasing the walls, echoed hints of a paradise now long lost under the progress of concrete and steel.

I was to meet my host, Mr Aoi Saito, at the top of the steps. He was to chauffeur me to my new home for the next year after guiding me on a brief tour of Haifuku Kawakami – a preview for my more in-depth reconnaissance the next day. He was of average height and weight with no special features apart from a wide smile rippling across his face and a light dancing in his eyes. Holding a sign with my name, he obviously had recognised me from my application photo. I bowed awkwardly and he shook my hand lightly. Then he ushered me into a nearby car so small and dainty it looked as if a light drizzle could crumple it.

We cruised slowly, never getting close to a faster speed. His English was almost flawless as he had studied in the US in his youth and had made a point of keeping the skill sharp ever since. While driving to my new home, he informed me I would have to use the bus for my daily commute, which, thankfully, the school would pay for. However, it was a less than convenient ten-minute walk to the bus stop (at a fast pace, he said). He noted that sudden sea storms can easily brew, wetting you through in the blink of an eye. I thought, silently, *this might develop into an annoyance!* He then showered me with a barrage of questions too trivial to mention, and I struggled to answer them with enthusiastic replies due to my travel fatigue. It was small talk without any weight of conviction, and I made the usual standard personal enquiries one does when meeting someone new.

Modest would not adequately describe my own private little enclave for the next year. Even humble would be wild praise. Severely austere just barely did it justice, and I doubt my best counterfeit smile hid my thoughts from my chaperon. I had, of course, expected practical Japanese smallness but with quality and ingenuity, something Japan was famous for. I was disappointed. The abstract dull decor and faceless furnishings depressed me. There was no colour or character – just sanatorium white. I stood there in the doorway barely remembering to slip my shoes off, as Japanese custom dictates and as my host Mr Aoi Saito did. He had repeated his name so frequently and dramatically, I will remember it till my last day. The sound of it may even invade my last exhale. I flicked the light switch and the room lit up with a loud buzz, which slowly petered off to a barely audible hum. The room looked as desolate in the light as in the dark. Mr Saito and I said our awkward farewells and agreed to meet in the morning.

The fridge had been helpfully stacked with Western microwave meals. In truth, I am very fond of this cardboard food. The one-room flat sported a corseted partition that could be pulled across to give the illusion of two. The toilet and shower were tucked away behind an unnaturally heavy door.

After noticing the large extractor fan in the bathroom corner, I concluded that the heavy door was there to prevent steam escaping and redecorating the flat's white walls in avenging black mould.

That first night I spent watching bad Japanese soap operas with terrible subtitles while eating a microwave roast dinner that tasted like lukewarm water even though it was packed with a huge variety of unintelligible compounds in the package's ingredient list. The rain punched the windowpanes as though begging to be let in. As I unrolled my futon in the fractional space between the wardrobe and computer desk, I wondered drearily what lay ahead. I hoped I would sleep soundly and not wake up in the dark to find myself tangled around the furniture just inches away.

Chapter Six

Haifuku Kawakami village, stretching over 4km, is literally a one-road town of just over 1,000 people. It clings to the banks of the Abu River, a 90-km waterway. It's a place so inconsequential that it's barely mentioned in the Prefecture guides and not even noted in local histories. Densely forested hills threateningly flank the back of the town, looking ready to swallow anyone daring to step off their meagre trails. The Abugawa Dam is on the inland edge of the town's boundary – a primary scenic spot. The Abu River History and Folklore Museum – the town's cultural highpoint and single attraction – is just before the dam with a canoeing centre, the solo activity, barely beyond. Two liquor stores, almost side by side, are the town's local amenities. A tiny one-room general store holds half its stock in the two outside vending machines. A prefab post office in the thralls of decay, and a small wooden Buddhist temple – *Gyokusenji* – are also in the village. I would soon realise such temples are almost obligatory in even the most minor of settlements. Dumped in the middle of the town are the Hagishiritsu Kawakami Elementary School and Hagishiritsu Kawakami Junior High School – my place of work for the next year. This building is a two-story prefab monstrosity of decaying grey-flaked paint and rusted window frames. The school uniform is a post-World War II drab blue, old-style sailor suit. The girls' versions are ankle-length skirts and loose-fitting blazers – quite the opposite to the miniskirts and tight shirts of the popular anime clichés.

After my arrival in Haifuku Kawakami, the first notable event took place in the town hall – the largest and most modern building in the town. Mr Aoi Saito introduced me to the mayor and other town dignitaries, including the shop owners and my fellow teachers. Thankfully, most could speak enough basic English to hold a light conversation, keeping awkward silences down to a minimum. Mr Aoi Saito was always at my side and could easily smooth over any lost-in-translation difficulties. The whole exercise was mildly pleasant yet instantly forgettable. Later, I was introduced to the pupils during a school assembly. The next day I began teaching.

ESID (Every Situation Is Different) is a term I have learnt to dread and will despise for the rest of my days. Like many acronyms, it is as hollow in its guidance as its practical application. I was soon to discover that neither life's training, professional JET courses, nor general life experiences will help you navigate the vague horrors within different situations.

Every teacher is a prophet, general, and emperor. Inside the four walls of their classroom, their word is law, their will absolute, their diktats unquestionable. This is especially true in Japan. I soon found I was an "assistant" in the loosest of senses as I had to create, plan, and teach the entire class on my own. My master, Mr Niko Nakajima, was always watching from the shadows of his desk, ready to pounce if a lesson went too far off track or the class boiled over to muffled hysteria.

My average daily schedule involved rising at 6:00a.m., an hour (in my opinion) alien to the civilised mind. I washed in my tiny, claustrophobia-inducing shower. The only way to fit in that space was to hunch over in such a way as to put Quasimodo to shame. Showered, I threw on my clothes and raced to the bus stop for my twenty-minute commute. After arriving at my destination, I quickly ate my breakfast in the teachers' lounge, building my resolve for the day ahead while muttering half-hearted greetings to my caffeine-tainted colleagues. Most days, these were the only moments of peace I would have before dragging myself to the school's front gate to meet my arriving students. The next few hours were packed with a blur of broken English activities laced with hyperactivity from repeating the alphabet to a few rounds of heads, shoulders, knees and toes. I also sometimes experienced long stoic hours playing on my phone in the teachers' lounge with nothing to do and no one to talk to while waiting for lunch, which I had to eat with the children. This wasn't fun. It was more work involving repeating basic questions for them to answer so they could practice their muddled English: What's your favourite colour? What sort of food do you like? What sport are you best at? This took place every lunch break five days each week. Depending on the day's lesson plan, it would either speed by in an instant at full throttle, leaving me almost crashing from exhaustion, or there would be so little to do I would be bored to the brink of senselessness. The day-to-day work could range from the extremes of monotony, to frenetic, to outright worrisome, totally depending on the day. Most students were interested in western music and comics more than really learning English.

In my down time, my mind often drifted back to my London JET interview. I sat fully suited opposite a panel of three former JET teachers in a lightly heated London office. I still felt chilled from the icy February wind roaring down the Thames as I walked to the appointment. This interview was the final hurdle. If I cleared it, I would be hired! The complimentary cup of processed coffee shavings in my hand did little to revive my frozen blood which, if nothing more, kept my senses on edge. The questions they asked turned out to be little more than regurgitations from the application. I gave answers fused with fake enthusiasm and admittedly questionable grammar as steadily as possible. I didn't want to sound too over-rehearsed. Soon, I realised the interview was nothing more than an over-glorified formality. The main qualities they seemed to be looking for were confidence and charm to glide over any obstacles that might fall in my path. Excellence in English grammar and language acquisition did not seem so important. Finally, after much mutual handshaking and back-slapping, my place was all but assured.

Chapter Seven

The first term was soon over. Spring was in her infancy and the first flowers of Japan's world-famous cherry blossoms blanketed the land. Thus far, the experience had neither been as tedious as expected nor as thrilling as hoped – instead, mediocre. On the other hand, my social life had taken on a more exciting edge. I soon found that being a local novelty had the advantage that everyone wanted to know you, if for nothing more than to practise their English. My minor ethnic celebrity status in the small town made my life there excessively easy. In a matter of weeks, I had settled into small-town life. The only real niggle was when people stared at me (especially elderly Japanese) as if I were a creature from another world. There also seemed to be a generally unhealthy interest in my grocery shopping habits. A minor annoyance was that in one of the most advanced countries on earth, people still pay almost one hundred per cent in cash for everything from a prepared lunch box to an envelope-busting wad to pay the rent. My adventures in the nearby city of Hagi on weekends had been more of the mature kind.

The town of Haifuku Kawakami was a tad on the dull side even during its busiest days, so you can imagine how at night it was dreary beyond belief, bereft of basic bars or restaurants for the mildest of entertainment. So all the hot young males like me, and even older, looking for more mature entertainment left for the Hagi at the slightest excuse.

Hagi is a historic castle city famous for its cultural richness. It claims no less than five UNESCO World Heritage sites, including an eighteenth-century reverberatory furnace, the first in the East able to cast cannons, and the Ebisugahana Shipyard, which build the ships that carry Japanese power to the world.

Hagi's political pedigree is no less impressive. It is the birthplace of three former prime ministers and boasts five nationally famous temples. One is in the large city centre, dedicated to the eighteenth-century revolutionary and godfather of the Meiji Restoration, Yoshida Shoin. Another, on the city's outskirts, is the small temple of Unrin-ji – solely dedicated to cats and their fanatical worshippers. The city is now cursed with a rapidly dwindling population from the lack of modern industry and a poor transport infrastructure. Left with only its historical relevance, the city is currently little more than a living museum.

Every Friday and Saturday night the young and the damned left Haifuku Kawakami. Some tried their luck in Hagi's neon bars, shaded night clubs and deafening karaoke booths. Others went to the smoother, laid-back jazz lounges, all tucked away within the historical Edo-period cityscape. The trip was less than an hour by bus. Fortunately, Hagi was the last stop on the route, so a quick siesta was often achievable. I had easily made friends with three of the teachers at my school. We were roughly the same age, wide-eyed with the wild fires of youth. Our other work colleagues seemed geriatric, life's inevitable grind long ago having dulled their spark for frivolous fun. Haruto and Minato had grown up in Haifuku Kawakami and returned straight after graduation from university. Yui used to live in Hagi, so he knew the best places to drink and – more importantly – had ample female friends for us to meet. Being white and English, two-thirds of the job of wooing was accomplished by my genetics and birthright.

Chapter Eight

For dramatic purposes, I will give an extremely condensed example of the deepest woes of my teaching experience. It's the only episode really worth mentioning – a bonfire of drama in a sea of mostly dreck and tedium. This happened on one of the many school trips we took. Japan has many more school trips than most other industrial nations, often varying in length, at a multitude of locations, and on a variety of themes.

Our spring trip from Haifuku Kawakami was an overnight camp in a nearby forest dominating the hills towering over the town. The dense canopy of those hills acted as backdrops for the gardens at some of the houses. The local folk museum and canoeing centre were unlikely activity bedfellows, one based on superstition, the other on activity. To the uninitiated, canoeing is one of the most impractical forms of exercise. The truth is that canoeing leads to little intellectual or physical advancement. It was clear they had both been chosen purely for the convenience of their nearby location than any real merit.

We set off from Haifuku Kawakami's back door on an early cool spring morning. We hiked up a twisting path, slipping between trees and around bushes. Our heavy equipment and luggage had been transferred the night before to the campsite.

The children carried their lunch; the teachers also carried theirs, supplemented with walkie-talkies and first-aid kits to cover any hazards, from plasters for scraped knees to alerting helicopters for children who had strayed and possibly fallen down chasms. We thought we were ready for every scenario our limited imaginations could think of.

The walk was gruelling but not because of the pace being too fast. Ironically, it was due to the extremely slow pace travelled in single file at the speed of the slowest child. The rambling speed could be due to the child's asthma and some other minor ailment. Or it could be caused by easily tempted minds wandering from the path to inspect every passing bright flower, follow each radiant dragonfly, or curiously investigate every rustle of foliage passed. The tree shade guarded against the midday heat. A soft breeze cooled us, and the walk would have been pleasant if not for the wandering and frequently squabbling children.

We arrived at the campsite lightly dusted and peppered with sweat as the trees filtered the sun's unrelenting glare. Thankfully, the cooking and commune mess tents were already set up. Various senior teachers prepared the evening meals and activities, leaving us JETS and junior teachers to corral the children into functioning groups to help them put their tents up – a task almost as practical as dictating to the stars. It took us to the limits of our patience and skill as over-excited children are as much use with their practical skills as a bear with chopsticks. After toiling for an hour, we finally finished setting up camp to a reasonable standard. This was a herculean task on a par with the Siege of Troy: it had the same chance of slipping into total chaos at a moment's notice.

With barely enough time to spare, we began the afternoon activities. The schedule had to be followed as rigidly as regimental orders. The first and primary activity on the programme was a visit to the Abu River History and Folklore Museum, which was a brisk walk down the hill and across the reservoir dam. Haifuku Kawakami could barely be seen just around the Abu River bend. To our left, we could see the Canoeing Centre – our target for the next day's morning activities up-river to our right.

The museum is a cluster of single-floor thatched-roof buildings. The roofs were painted aqua green and padded with generations of thick moss. The buildings were surrounded by a weaved wooden ribbon fence, snagged by rot and age. They sat in the mouth of a shallow valley, miles from any other buildings, a lost outpost in the style of the last century. A long row of heavily eroded Buddha statues greeted us, their facial features long scrubbed off by the elements, leaving only an eerie faceless sheen. The car park's concrete was a mass of deep spider-web cracks. Chipped off chunks rattled as the children kicked them before they skidded off into the unkempt grass and ragged bushes.

The museum's interior was immaculate compared to the shabby outside. As we entered, we found that the left wall was dedicated to the general history of the river, starting in antiquity when it was a simple trade route for all the outlying villages. The river leads straight into the centre of Hagi; its banks were too quick to flood, the rolling hills too steep to pave. It was only when the dam was built in 1970 that the by-then dwindling maritime tradition of hand-paddled haulage and light fishing finally came to an end. There were various black-and-white photos from the turn of the century featuring rickety boats surrounded by gap-toothed peasants, their wares piled high, their keels dipping low. The explanations were solely in Japanese, but I doubt that an English translation would have made the subject any more fascinating. I suspect that few subjects are as dull to children and adults alike.

On the other hand, the opposite wall seemed to hold the children's attention like a vice, an impressive feat even in optimum classroom circumstances and unheard of the moment the little dears are away from the vortex drag of the blackboard. These display pictures were in full, detailed colour, unlike their sibling's grey tones, and it was clear this was the museum's main attraction and centrepiece. Alas, all text was again only in Japanese, so the subtle nuances were lost on me, though I could follow the general gist.

The pictures told various folklore stories, from nationally famous tales to local stories about the surrounding valley towns, as Japan is woven together from a tapestry of two millenniums of countless fables, all eternal, always evolving. It is woven from tale threads made famous through anime to worldwide audiences, or local stories stitched together in oral retellings, or lore in neglected musty tomes forgotten on the bottom shelves in local libraries, or, as in this case, pinned to fraying poster boards in a building a mild tremor away from complete collapse.

Of what I could follow through the faded-edged panels, the most popular local tale was about a spirit of nature that switched between a fox and wolf depending on the circumstances. This spirit acted as a moral guardian of the local woods and valleys. In its fox form, the spirit would help lost children find their way back to the path or scare off gluttonous crows for the humble farmer. In wolf form, it would savage wayward poachers and chase off overly enthusiastic, wasteful lumberjacks. The moral was as subtle as a sledgehammer and about as practical for modern life's dilemmas. All this was illustrated with pictures, switching from cute and placid to brutal and gory in a panel. There was not even the slightest pretence of a moral grey area.

We finally left the museum and trudged back to camp across the spine of the dam before scaling the hill. To our group of little-legged explorers, we may well have been ascending the steep side of Mount Everest given the jarring whines growing with every metre climbed. Soon, the whines and the huffing and puffing were laced with tears. We bribed the children with handfuls of biscuits and copious amounts of orange juice, which seemed to settle their spirits, and the threatening drama of the hour was soon forgotten when the land levelled out. We then engaged in some light activities, including a short circular nature walk, which in the dimming light seemed rather pointless as the shadows cloaked even the largest critters the children might have been able to see. Of course, that's if their chatter had not already scared those animals away. Finally, around the campfire, the children sang so joyfully, loud and out of tune, I was surprised the racket didn't wake the last three generations of their ancestors with alarmed horror. Thankfully, it was soon time for bed. We crawled into our sleeping bags, knowing that by the same time tomorrow we would be back in our own beds in civilisation.

A deep, panicked screaming shook me awake. It was plain what the emergency was – there was no need for explanation. The loss of a child in any circumstance is a dread crossing every culture. I quickly dressed and staggered out to where the other teachers were already searching in their designated areas. They pointed to my own.

A dense fog had ambushed us during the night. Its atmosphere muted our shouts and distorted our torch beams. As the fog swirled around my feet, I walked blindly, tripping on tree roots and slipping off rocks with every other step. The base theory was that we either had a sleepwalker or the child had got disoriented looking for the toilet. In this fog, there was a greater chance of him stumbling into the mystical city of El Dorado or falling down the mountainside and breaking his neck than finding his own way back to camp, especially when, like all children, he was close to the ground in a foreign realm, making disorientation almost inevitable. After fifteen minutes of laborious searching, made more difficult by the night fog, all the worst-case scenarios had raced through my mind, growing more alarming and grotesque by the moment. Suddenly, I heard a cry on the wind, which forced my mind back to reality. I hurried in the general direction of the sound.

The moon had emerged from behind the clouds. Maybe out of guilt or a weak show of friendship to my cause, the fog now lit into a cloudy glow and the plaintive cry led me on. Blinded by the fog, my eyes were next to useless. My ears were the only sense left that was worth a damn.

A shadow emerged slowly out of the fog. It was coiled in the foetal position on the ground. I hesitantly approached, hoping to be rewarded with the missing boy. Instead, a slim trail of blood led my way. I almost lost my footing in terror.

Torn flesh strips littered each side of the blood trail, and with macabre curiosity, I reached down to pick up one of the pieces. One side was fuzzy. Horrified that it was possibly the child's shredded scalp in my hand, my stomach stirred, on the verge of vomiting. Now I was almost on top of the corpse. I knelt down to find a mass of white curls I assumed to be the child's jacket. I rolled the body over to find the marble black eyes of a lamb staring back. Looking around the area as I exhaled a breath of deep relief, I saw the outline of a child's discarded shoe. It was like a tracking sign, its toe leading me on my own private scavenger hunt. A child's life hung in the balance, which could soon end in a miracle or tragedy.

I picked up and studied the shoe, finding it damp to my touch. I rubbed the liquid on the shoe between my fingers, looking closely. It was clear. I guessed it was early morning dew, no doubt birthed from the plastic imitation leather. The shoe was infused with flakes of grit and grime but, thankfully, no traces of wet or clotted blood. I pressed on, remembering the ripped lamb's death gaze now forever upon the stars, its body stiff with the night's cold, its life taken by a predator in a momentary lapse of attention. The fog seemed to be thinning – or perhaps my eyes had finally adjusted to it. Either way, I pushed on towards the sound of the crying, which seemed to have taken on a harsher, lower tone. It was more like a deep growl than a child's plea.

I came to a small clearing spotlighted by the pale moon's glow. I was witnessing the unfolding of either triumph or tragedy. A small bundle of limbs lay curved on the ground. The twitching head and soft shuffles were the indistinguishable movements of a child held in the vicelike fear of no-escape. Three large shadows circled, their claws tapping on the shale, the air muffled by their low growls. I picked up a nearby tree branch. I inhaled deeply and then stormed forward, shouting in lung-rupturing decibels. I half expected to be ripped and gored to death in moments, hopefully giving enough time for the boy to escape an expensive funeral and receiving local immortality as my reward.

For a second, seven pairs of eyes turned on me, six wild ones and the child's innocent ones pleading for help. I was ready to use my branch as a baseball bat to take out at least one of my slayers with me. I hung in the balance between life and death for a fraction of a moment. All I had ever done in the last twenty-two years leading to this experience was what washed over me in my rush of narcissistic bravery.

The beasts raced towards me. As they advanced, their shadows grew and their statures shrank. The fog had distorted and magnified their forms and growls, yet I kept on edge to the last instant until they scattered into the forest. None of the foxes had been larger than a medium-size mutt. I scooped the screaming boy into my arms, walked back to camp and put him to bed. The next morning the whole episode was nothing more to him than a vivid nightmare, forgotten by the time his parents picked him up.

Chapter Nine

Soon summer, its blaze of colourful flora and warmth burnt out, was replaced by winter with its unforgiving icy sheen and snow cloak. Japan celebrates Christmas despite being less than one per cent Christian. It is a minor holiday before the major event of the new year. Christmas is actually for couples. It is by far Japan's most romantic day of the year on par with Valentine's Day in the West. At Christmas, the streets are lined with fairy lights and (if you can believe it) the main meal is KFC – a holy tradition started after a 1970 ad series. Reservations are required months ahead. In the evening, children exchange gifts that are opened neatly and slowly, taking care to keep the wrapping paper intact. Quite different from the Western kinetic ripping frenzy! Thus, the typical atheist Japanese festival, absent of Jesus Christ, now has more in common with its modern, Western bastardisation than should be religiously tolerable.

I did not travel home for Christmas. Truth is, I wanted to avoid my parents' disappointment with my choice to teach in Japan. Social media's constant digital waterfall meant I could follow my few real friends and many casual acquaintances in real time perhaps easier than returning home. The odd social media emojis and comments were enough to make them aware of my presence. Their replies of curiosity and envy were my private festive sparks.

I had managed to fit into my new teaching routine better than some of my colleagues, whose escapades I had been following on Facebook and various message boards threaded together with a mishmash of internet blogs. These made me aware of things like the shockingly low age of consent of thirteen and the disturbing ritual of teachers inspecting teenage schoolgirls' underwear to confirm they were only wearing white. They had to bunch their knickers round their ankles for them to check for "cleanliness". Then there was the bizarre tradition of pupils cleaning their classrooms and toilets daily and the harsh school lunch policy of healthy food only. No food could be brought from home, and this rule is strictly enforced with random bag inspections.

There were stories running the gauntlet from being sniggeringly silly to disturbing and shocking. One was about a girl so lovestruck with Japan's natural assets while out cycling in the mountainous countryside that she failed to read the steep road signs and crashed her way straight into a six-month hospital stay. Another was about a JET teacher who got not just one, but two high school girls pregnant. Still another concerned a JET teacher who got arrested for sucking off a thirteen-year-old boy in a public restroom. Most wondered if both episodes were in the same class or even the same school district. I was stunned to hear these stories. Other tales were more drearier than dreadful, like the weeb girl who insisted on using a Japanese name just because it was cool. Her love for all things anime and manga was so great that she spent nearly every weekend in the nearest larger city devouring all the anime stores and cafés. Sacrificing her chance to forge friendships with her pupils and colleagues, she spent her weekday time alone wallowing in her own warped hubris.

***

I met Sakura (Japanese for "cherry blossoms", which she matched in both looks and personality) on a lazier-than-normal Saturday spring night just shy of ten months into my placement. In retrospect, our meeting seemed preordained. It occurred in a bar called Lounge Love – a den of legal vice and heavy liquor in the spirit of Dionysus. Lounge Love is a temple of red leather seats, marble-black walls and blue mood lighting. It sits on the Matsumoto River, which winds through Hagi. I was amusing my small, enthralled group of new friends with anonymous tales of malice and disgust from my fellow expats. The group consisted of Haruto, Minato, Yui and two of his friends. One of his friends – Sakura – soon caught my eye, and I would find out the next morning that I had captured her attention instantly. In the evening's easy haze, we had waltzed from bar to bar, finding them strangely half-empty. As if in some twist of fate, our small group was the only centre of attention for the night. Since going to a deserted nightclub makes as much sense as pirouetting through a graveyard at dawn, we ended up in an all-night restaurant where the loudest noise was the clinking of glasses.

A large amount of sake – Japan's primer alcoholic inhibitor – had eroded my self-control and wasted away Sakura's morals. It allowed us to drunkenly skip back to her flat for some shameless shenanigans. This climaxed in two hours of early-morning sex, which got better each time as we sobered up. As the hours slid by, high levels of caffeine and sugar pushed us on, keeping us awake, letting us sweat out our hangovers, and inviting us to continue what adults naturally do when they are naked. When we finally fell asleep, exhausted, it was deep and dreamless. It was well into Sunday afternoon when we stirred.

As is often the case in these first-encounter hook-up situations, we knew nothing practical about each other apart from what we learnt the night before through cocktails, casual flirting and light banter. So as we talked, I learnt that she was a customer manager at a large shopping mall and had worked herself up from a shop assistant. She had forsaken university for reasons she did not want to elaborate on. The mounting awkwardness told me she clearly felt the need to change the conversation. I looked over a cluster of photos almost covering a far wall. To my surprise, a number of them showed her by the sea in her primary school days. The background was stunning, totally barren of any man-made structures. When I asked her about the location of this isolated cove, which appeared untouched by human hands, she said it was a full day's walk from a remote, rural train station, and she had visited there when young with her father. She added that her grandfather had once lived and worked in the village before the "incident". I could tell by her demeanour, a disturbance washing over her face, that she did not want to elaborate. Thankfully, I was soon hard again. When she noticed, her eyes lit up. It was the perfect excuse to put the topic to bed for the time being, washed away with unbridled lust. Before leaving each other that afternoon, we exchanged phone numbers and agreed to meet again. We had almost unknowingly fallen into a relationship. At first, we only saw each other on weekends in Hagi due to work and travel time. Indeed, it was more entertaining and less conspicuous than Haifuku Kawakami's single street. We usually shared an evening meal, then I stayed over Saturday night at her place before returning to Haifuku Kawakami Sunday afternoon. Almost unnoticeably, we began texting each other more, and Saturday sleepovers soon became all-weekend affairs. Before long, the whole teaching term had passed. I had never forgotten the cove picture on her wall, and after a fair amount of persistent pestering, Sakura finally agreed to take me on the train to Nago village. From there we would hike to Modoro Cape. It would be an excuse for a romantic weekend away for her and a chance for me to scuba dive properly in the beautiful waves, something I had not done since arriving in Japan.

After buying some cheap camping gear and renting standard scuba gear, we set off early Friday morning for our adventure.

Chapter Ten

The Nago train station, less than an hour from Hagi, is one of the most basic imaginable in Japan. It's a small brick building with a rusted iron roof and wood-panelled waiting room which has not changed since its 1929 construction. The station is used mostly for daily travel to school for the various farm children and general commuters travelling to Hagi and beyond. Thus, it is really only busy at peak times and weekends. The few compulsory vending machines outside the station were the only hint of the modern world. Apparently you can find vending machines in every corner and crevice of Japan regardless of population density or practicality. They are so abundant, you wonder if when the Japanese reach the moon, their first act will be to install a vending machine dispenser. The train pulled away with a great rattling, leaving just Sakura and myself on the platform in a small hamlet with only wilderness for company.

Nago is a rural town even smaller than Haifuku Kawakami. It's a blip in the valley between Hagi and Masuda, its streets trailing each side of two rivers – the Go and the Nagoya. The town has no less than four religious institutions – two Buddhist temples, one Shinto shrine, and a new religion called

Tenrikyo, founded by Nakayama Miki in the seventeenth century, a mystic prophet little known outside Japan. Apart from a fishing tackle shop, a café and a small convenience store, there are only a few small side streets filled with houses. The oddness of having more religious sites then practical amenities was not lost on me. There was little else in Nago other than a patchwork of farms sheltered by rolling hills, which we were soon to ascend. Conquering the horizon in front of us was a backdrop of densely wooded valleys.

Our route for the coming day would be starting on Nago's outskirts before climbing over a few hills to our mid-destination, Takamine Shrine, near the largest hill's peak. Then we would drop down to our final destination near Modoro Cape, a former fishing village with a tale of mysterious destruction that I hoped Sakura would soon enlighten me about.

On the edge of Nago, we found our starting point: the narrow road passing the Daikakuji Buddhist Temple with its large, centuries-old trees twisted by time and weathered stone Buddhas, their eyes millennium wise. The brilliant white temple, almost too dazzling to look upon, sits at the top of moss-encrusted stairs. To the side, we noticed a few aged narrow tombstones, so old they had partially crumbled back into Earth's embrace.

The road soon petered off into a footpath, narrowing with every passing metre of our climb till it became a barely visible gravel slither beckoning us into the forest. The shade of the dense trees soon cooled the warm summer air. Light came at a premium. The forest's thick canopy shade cloaked the sky's light and blocked the horizon, leaving us generally disoriented. Even with a path leading the way, we were glad for our compass confirming our direction. A barrage of unseen birds tweeted, mocking us from above, their songs echoing in stereo.

It was clear that the path was not well used. I was told that only the odd, curious day-tripper and melancholy relative made the pilgrimage we had now embarked upon. In anywhere else in the world, such scenery would be used as an infinite treasury. Cafés would be present, serving tea to elderly couples. Paved footpaths would be laid to keep packed coaches of townies from getting mud on their expensive, impractical trainers. Fences would frame the road to contain an elaborately named natural park with pay and display parking fees to see Mother Nature's abundant privileges. But to the Japanese, with their hundreds of miles of unblotched treescapes and coastline, Nago background hills were nothing more than small hills too rugged and remote to be worth building on.

When we finally mounted the ridge, the wind ambushed and bombarded us with heavy pollen. Now we only needed to follow its shallow spine to its higher siblings, the forest's grip thinning, weakened by the steep embankments and shallow earth, the sun relentlessly bleeding down from its midday throne. We drank deeply and frequently. The hours slipped by as the Takamine Shrine slowly crawled towards us.

The shrine sat just before the peak in the crease of a small clearing. It was almost level on its own private plateau about the size of a quarter of a football pitch. It looked like a flat dimple flacked by shear slopes. We sat for some lunch, noticing how the farmland ran like ribbons down to the valley's base before being cut by the coastline and finally halted by the sea. Unlike most shrines in Japan, which have the illusion of regular care and attention, any upkeep here was at a minimum. Being so high, remote and exposed, no doubt this shrine made even the most basic maintenance a mammoth task.

The Torii Gate, standing alone, separated the Shinto shrine from the mundane world. It was necessary to pass under the gate to transcend to the sacred realm. The gate looks like an upside down "U" with an extra line across its peak, yet it sat crooked, its left side sunk at least a foot into the mud. The *sandō*, or main path, was covered by shattered *tōrō* stone lanterns long fallen from their pedestals. The sprawling green moss clutching the paint was a testament to the gate's abandonment. A pair of serious, lion-like stone statues guarded the remains of an inner shrine, called the *hoden*, now nothing more than a dull brick building the size of a large shed. The grim statues sat there to ward off evil spirits. Called *Komainu* in Japanese, they had a lion's proud body and small dog's squat-faced head. Their once-ferocious teeth and piercing eyes had long since crumbled and cracked, replacing their formerly graced workmanship with a featureless farce. The *kami* resides in this shrine. It is the dedicated nature spirit, neither good nor evil, the essence of the mountain where it had dwelled long before the unified nation state or the footsteps of men.

We ate our lunch outside the shrine under the weak shade of an old, twisted tree deformed by decades of exposure to tearing winds. It was quiet. Nothing moved: no bugs, no birds. This was in stark contrast to our climb up the hill, which had been filled with scurrying, furry critters in our path and a battle with pesky bugs. Who knows why? Perhaps the Shrine's absent greenery and merciless wind was nature's way of discouraging wildlife.

We had finished our lunch. It was getting late, so we hastily left the shrine. After a brief climb to the final peak, we started down on our four-hour journey to the fishing village at Modoro Cape. The steep downward trek left our calf muscles screaming and our knees buckling. After reaching the bottom, we flitted between the valley trees until we saw the faint glow of the coast greeting us. Whispering winds carried the strong scent of sea salt and screeching of seagulls, reminding us we were their guests, nothing more. Our tired legs pushed forward to the top of the last small rise separating us from our final destination. Finally, we saw the abandoned town below, beckoning us like a dilapidated Shangri-La.

It was a one-street town sitting in a shallow valley. For the most part, only a few small, ramshackle house-shells stood upright. The valley curved down to a dip in the cliff line, finally breaking out into a natural harbour that wound around the shoreline. The cliffsides acted as walls, forming a natural barrier against the elements. In the late eighteenth to early nineteenth centuries, the settlement had been nothing more than a layover and supply stop to more exciting destinations.

The cove was often used for waiting out the violent storms that rolled in from the unpredictable Sea of Japan without a moment's notice. Mostly, sea travellers used the town as a stopping-off point when night-time sea travel was too hazardous for small vessels. We noticed the remains of what looked like a sailing essentials store and a small, rickety inn. Most likely, it had doubled as a brothel for the sailors, serving their carnal desires and offering intoxicating refreshment.

Our first task was to set up camp at the neck the valley. From our tent porch, we could look down on the dilapidated village about half a mile away with the sea as its backdrop. The tent was a simple affair, and my previous experience at one too many music festivals meant erecting it was only a half-hour job. Japan isn't big into camping culture – the "civilised" world's last chance to pit itself against the unforgiving chaos of nature. This is the opposite of standard Japanese culture, where people must follow behaviour rules from cradle to grave to avoid bringing ridicule and shame to their families. Sakura found the illicit thrill of wild camping an exhilarating rebellion against those rules.

We had brought only the raw basics for weight and simplicity. Chemically flavoured dried noodle pots and a mixed bag of fresh fruit was our only food. Our drinking water was limited, so we were lucky to find a small fresh stream running down the central crease of the valley that we could purify with a light boil and some iodine droplets.

Chapter Eleven

The red-orange sun was beginning to set, leaving less than two hours of thinning light. After collecting our water ration for the night, we returned to the abandoned village to walk among the town ruins framed by growing shadows of dying light. The smell of rotten wood peppered and preserved with sea salt greeted us long before we were close enough to focus on anything other than vague forms. We followed a stone path headed into the town, polished by generations of sailors and partially blanketed over by moss. This made traction in our well-treaded trainers difficult at times. As we approached the edge of the town, the few standing buildings had black, barbequed edges so decrepit I was sure it was only the vines intertwining around them that held them vertical. All Japanese buildings of that age had been made of wood, so it took very little imagination of how an intense, brutal firestorm raging through the village would have consumed it in no time, leaving only the sparse, littered remains greeting us now.

There was an unnatural stillness. I noticed it as soon as we entered the town through a still-standing, half-rotted traditional Japanese archway. Once inside, we noticed how all outside sound seemed to cease – even the deafening chirruping of crickets was oddly absent. I guessed the soft, raw, exposed cliffs sheltering the remaining walls were absorbing their noise, reflecting it back into the sea. Still, there was something mildly unsettling at the silence.

In the fading light, we noticed how the few standing building struts of the once-proud tavern – the hamlet's sole social forum – were infested with seemingly millions of mites. Their tiny, almost transparent bodies scuttled around absently. The wreckage of once-proud bird nests littered the area like gravestones, holding the tiny bones of fragile baby birds, sometimes two or three layers thick. I figured the nests had fallen from a crease in the cliffs above. A soft gust of wind made the fragile bones rustle and rattle like tiny wind chimes. The intermittent light from cloud breaks sent shadows to dance on the bleached chalk cliff walls. It felt like a macabre shadow puppet show.

Finally, we came to the beach edge. The area had once been a natural harbour, a mouth at night inhaling weary crews, tired from the toil of voyage, then a day later exhaling them fresh-faced and resupplied. The harbour's lime bedrock wore a black cloak showing a glass-like polish, probably from the heat of some violent fire that had reached the cove, its flames goaded by strong winds. An inferno that had grasped and crushed the whole hamlet in its fist of fury.

We sat on the beach contemplating the possibility, then stood up. As we headed back to camp, I saw a small Shinto cemetery in a shallow dip halfway between the town and our campsite. It had rows of oblong marks, faded carved letters marking its inhabitants. It was almost camouflaged by the thick, knee-high grass – a testament to what had been the total destruction of the village population. No ancestor was left to attend to the graves. Long-extinguished stone lamps lay topsy-turvy throughout the area. In a few more decades – a generation at most – I suspected the whole tragedy of this sad little town would be remembered only as an episode of Japan's rich folklore.

We returned to our camp in the late dusk underneath rising stars and falling temperature. Safe inside our tent overlooking the sea, we felt the rippling wind flicking the tent's outer skin like waves. We peeked out the door flaps to see a few hints of boats on the horizon, their lights bobbing on the sea waves. They looked like tiny tin and steel capsules enclosed in their own micro-universe just as we were in our tiny nylon tent on the hill. We pulled the flaps back down to keep the wind out and the heat in. Then, on the tent's temporary porch – despite a large "no fire" symbol telling us not to do so – we boiled water over a small stove to make our dehydrated feast. A small torch we had clumsily strung to a plastic hook on the top of the inner tent swayed back and forth with each gust of wind as we hungrily ate our normally unappetising meal.

It was dark and we were full, so we climbed into our sleeping bag, eager to greet and warm each other up. Almost instantly after our brief moans of sexual pleasure had subsided, I began to hear noises – so many and variable as to comprise a vaguely disconcerting symphony.

Maybe it was Sakura's high-pitched squealing or my basstone moaning that had attracted the voyeur creatures, great and small. Still, humble truth be told, more than likely they had always been there, just overwhelmed by other daylight noises. As the sunlight slowly slipped away, their chatter concentrated around our private nylon colosseum, protecting us as we engaged in the most ancient of sports.

What instruments were in this odd orchestra? First, the loudly chirping crickets ramped up their mating calls, outstripping ours. Then, swallows flapping overhead in subtle whispers added to the mix. The sea's roaring waves, whipped on by a new night wind, completed the unholy symphony. I couldn't fall asleep from the noise. Until now, my camping experience had been limited to music festivals. There, I was used to being one among thousands where the chorus of snoring, shagging and vomiting under a star-addled night had brought a familiar comfort. So I was ill-prepared to cope with Mother Nature's sounds. Every leaf passing, every small mammal rattled jolted me into awareness, heart jumping, mind stammering. Ancient Neanderthal skills developed to guard against all threats had apparently mixed with my current hard-wired suspicion of the dark in an unknown place to keep me awake, commanding my body to do anything except sleep.

Chapter Twelve

I was curious about the events that had led to the town's fiery demise. Was it a case of mischievous fate or malicious arson? A stray lightning strike or a purposely struck match? My companion did not want to talk about it, which meant that if I brought up the subject, even subtly, she replied with a double-barrelled cold stare and quick verbal flick to change the subject. Still, the situation enticed me. I had now seen the carnage first hand. I think the mix of my nagging persistence and Sakura's close proximity to the tragedy finally pushed her to tell me the story (I may slightly elaborate on her version for dramatic purposes).

***

Most first-hand witnesses to the tale burned in the fire, and the few who lived scattered away to live with distant relatives. The story's pure truth has no doubt been stretched and distorted over the years by faltering memory and titillating hearsay. So the actual truth of the tale is anyone's guess. Only the bare-bone facts come close to anything like reliable. So here they are.

Inaka's fate was sealed by a violent storm that had forced a merchant ship into its harbour for an unscheduled stay. It had been carrying supplies for an upcoming celebration in Hagi, just under ten miles around the coast from Inaka. The storm was by far the worst in living memory, and history books would mark it as the tempest of the century. The harbour waves roared with the fury of a boiling cauldron. Only the bay's shallowness prevented the water's momentum from grabbing the ship and shattering it to oblivion against the cliff like a toddler carelessly tossing away a toy.

The merchant ship careened into the harbour, dodging rocks from the port side and slipping past fishing boats on the starboard side. It skidded up to the pier in a spew of sea froth. The crew collapsed. The sailors were on the verge of nervous convulsions, stressed and strained from wrestling the ship to safety. The severe tension had wrung life out of every sailor. All except one.

A reliable description of that sailor is lost to history. Still, it is known that he was from the north, as far north as Japan's Hokkaidō Island, where the snow clings to the peaks three-fourths of the year and the ice in the deepest valleys never truly thaws. He had escaped to sea when he was only a little older than a boy, orphaned by circumstances lost to time. He travelled the Asia seas for a decade, seeing more sights and having more adventures in a month than most people had in a lifetime.

Like all men, he had been physically and mentally sculpted by events in his life. He caught this little humdrum town's imagination. Why? Most had never left the area, often living and dying in the same house, a cycle reaching over the generations. So the people of the town could only stare in wonder at this sailor and his exotic clothes as he surged up the jetty, his swagger almost as infectious as his smile. The ship's explosive entrance into the harbour only enhanced his mystic aura.

There was only one tavern on the town's dockside. The group that greeted the sailor escorted him into the building while keeping their distance as though fearing an exotic animal. The rest of the crew was so sodden by the storm their sea legs gave out once they touched land. They couldn't follow and instead flopped into their bunks the moment the ship was securely anchored. At the same time, the captain drank from a bottle to abate his adrenaline jitters.

The tavern was crowded, heaving with gawking townspeople, some spilling out into the street. Despite all being from Japan, he seemed so foreign to these isolated locals that he could have come from a far-flung land from the other side of the globe. Like hypnotized moths, they flocked around as he smoked a fine ivory pipe leaving an intoxicating, smoky cloud. As he sat on a small, crooked stool – a majestic throne to the awed group – his rugged scent filled the room.

First, he set out to ease their small-town minds. He detected undisguised hostility in some who feared unknown foreigners. He decided that the best way to put their minds at ease would be to show his wealth. A generous and honest man, he paid for a round of drinks of strong sake for everyone – the first of many that night. While this small act of kindness gained him some respect and mild admiration, the evening's main course was just about to begin.

From his pocket, he produced two boxes: one of polished ivory, the other of scuffed wood. The ivory box was decorated with elephant figures. Ironically, the ivory construction material was made from the live elephants killed to provide it. The box contained the fuel for his well-used pipe, its smoke beguiling the group with its exotic scent. The second box was wooden. It was battered, worn, unpolished and unloved. He spilled its contents onto his hands, shuffling it from one hand to the other in an enticing manner. When he asked the people huddled around him if they would like a demonstration of the cosmic power he held in his hands, he was not short of volunteers.

There were twenty-four cards in his hands, their edges scuffed and rough. A tapestry of fingerprints blurred but could not totally eclipse the bright pictures on them. One showed a man sitting on a throne of gold holding a crowned sceptre in his hands. Another revealed a black-cloaked skeleton with a hard-edged sickle hanging from his shoulder. He sat on a decaying horse. Still another was a bizarre a picture of a ram-headed creature sitting on a throne of cracked bones holding a leash around the necks of a bowing naked man and woman. The people responded to the tarot cards with a mixture of glee and confusion. After passing them around, the sailor asked who wanted him to read their future.

An almost-toothless man volunteered first. The sun had baked his well-aged skin to a deep mahogany. His fingers were a patchwork of callouses earned by a lifetime of outdoor heavy labour. He was long past a dignified retirement age yet still far from useless as his main role in the community was fixing the fishermen's nets. Indeed, he was a living accumulation of a lifetime of experience and knowledge and thought he had seen it all. Nothing scared him anymore. After all, he was so old and close to death, what could possibly threaten him? He was a fool for believing that. He picked three cards from the sailor's hand.

The tavern's atmosphere was feverishly hot. Everyone watched in anticipation while the sailor turned over the cards, his pipe fumes feeding their delirium.

The first card showed a tower, its turret broken in half by lightning, its occupants falling in despair. The next card featured a chariot pulled by two sphinxes – one jet black, the other white as fresh snow. The third card showed two naked bodies woven together by a two-headed snake. The old man was dumbstruck. The audience was bemused as the art style and writing on the cards were unlike any they had ever seen. They waited with bated breath for the sailor to describe the volunteer's personal fate. He began his revelations in a hushed tone, heavy with prophecy:

'The tower card represents change. Whether good or bad, the path you choose is your own; the other cards may help guide you to your destiny. The next card shows the chariot, which represents the need to unwaveringly push forward. Only then can you overcome any challenges, regardless of the consequences. The last card, the lovers card, means you're at a crossroads – one path leading to ecstasy, the other to despair.'

Of course, we know now that tarot cards are, at best, nothing more than guides of what might happen if all goes uncharacteristically well. They aren't heaven-sent diktats of the future. Yet the sailor explained them as though to be stone-cold facts, a science developed in the Far West to map futures dictated by fate, not personal actions. After downing the dregs of his tea, the old man, dazed, walked away. He realised that he had lived his long life as nothing more than a naive follower of social morals and codes, as though his whole life had run on preordained tracks.

The second volunteer for the tarot card reading was opposite the first in both age and demeanour. Educated and somewhere between the middle and upper class, he was unsuperstitious and believed he was immune to trickery. He was a merchant who viewed the world through the cold logic of supply and demand, leaving no place for mystic hokum. Yet despite this, he was half-intrigued, half-determined to show the exotic guest's fakery, his cards a farce, to all others present. With these predispositions whirling in his mind, he chose his cards while gently sipping his tea.

The first card was a man hanging upside down by his feet from a tree branch, a look of deep peace set in his eyes. The second card was the picture of a circle floating in the clouds, its edges marked by strange symbols. The last card, easily recognised by everyone past and present, showed the sun beaming down on a grass meadow where a child was riding a horse. The merchant waited, slightly curious, for the sailor to read the meaning of his peculiar cards. The sailor's pipe smoke stung the merchant's eyes:

'The first card is the hanged man. This could either represent being suspended in time, total surrender, or being too scared to push on. The second card is the Wheel of Fortune. This brings major life changes, such as the rich becoming poor or the poor becoming rich. The final card showing the sun is one of the most optimistic tarot cards. It represents the universe coming together and agreeing with your path and aiding forward movement into something much greater.'

The merchant shuffled off his stool, picking out tea seeds trapped between his teeth. His swagger had drained. He appeared haunted, no longer the halcyon star of certainty. At first moving slowly, he soon began to rush as he fled the tavern into the embrace of the night.

It was late, the lanterns dim. The crowd began to thin as dawn stirred. After seeing the shattered looks and gelded pride of the sailor's first two volunteers, there were unsurprisingly few subsequent takers. Some stared down into their glasses into a safer, private universe. Others looked out tavern windows blackened by lamp oil. All seemed to be suffocating in the billows of the sailor's pipe smoke.

Then, softly and unsurely, a woman approached from the back of the room to volunteer. Her features were tidy, her eyes downcast. Her youth – in full bloom and easily seen, even in the dimming light – was reflected in the sake-dulled expressions of the few remaining patrons. The heavy eyelids of the tired sailor fluttered as he shuffled his cards and brewed his last cup of tea to christen the night's final hurrah.

The first card the sailor turned up was a shoeless man prancing towards a cliff edge, his frock jacket bellowing. He held his head high in ignorance with a bindle slung over his shoulder. The second card was a woman dressed in a white robe riding on a circlet of weaved gold. A pair of large feather wings protruded from her back. She held a gold cup in each hand, pouring water between them. The last card she chose was by far the strangest. It pictured a mass of naked people looking skywards at a female-winged torso bathed in clouds, its head blowing into a long gold tube. The girl sipped her tea as she waited for an explanation. She was too tired from work to show any hint of anticipation or terror. The host began to talk in a gently hushed tone.

'The first card is the Fool. This represents new beginnings and having faith in the future. The second card is Temperance, meaning that you should learn to bring about balance, patience and moderation in your life. The third card is Judgement, foreseeing a time of resurrection and awakening, a time when your current life comes to an end to make way for dynamic new beginnings.'

The young woman blinked and tried to cover a mighty yawn, her eyes heavy. Her mind was light from the constant flow of the sailor's thick smoke blowing at her like an asthmatic dragon. She bowed politely and thanked him before wandering into the dusk, where the storm had transitioned into a light tempest.

With no more volunteers for his tarot card readings, the sailor quickly and methodically packed away his cards. The others who remained rose, heavily drink-sodden into alcohol euphoria till the next night. They wearily pulled their coats tight, hoping to defend against the outside rain, but there was no physical or mental shield strong enough to protect them from their past misfortunes and possible future slights. The sailor was the last to leave, but he didn't return to his ship. Even his love for the sea had its limits. Unswaying land was now a novel pleasure, letting him reminisce about his almost-forgotten childhood of innocence on the crisp, pure shores of Hokkaidō before the dirty and glamorous ports of East Asia seeped and sullied his every pore. He chuckled softly to himself as he climbed the stairs of the tavern to the small room of his temporary lodging for the night. It was barren and bland, soon to be forgotten like a thousand others. The only difference was the girl from his third reading waiting by the door.

***

Outside, the storm continued, preventing the ship from leaving the harbour. In the morning, the sailors who had stayed on the vessel dispersed into the town, almost doubling its population. A few went into the tavern. Others wandered in the surrounding valley's fields, glad to be surrounded by a sea of solid green for a change as opposed to a delicate wooden ship in freezing water, which could be sunk a thousand different ways – from captain's error to nature's whim.

The next day a commotion started late afternoon as a mob from the town dragged the old man – the sailor's first volunteer for the tarot card reading – into the harbourmaster's office. It doubled as the town jail, the master himself also serving as mayor. He was one of the few fully educated members of the town. The old man, who the day before had been steady and reliable from the moment of his birth, was now wild, his mannerisms unkept, his eyes darting erratically and shaking in their sockets. Also with the old man was the sailor's second volunteer, the merchant, furious and foaming at the mouth, hollering for justice and waving his arms like a raving lunatic. The harbourmaster sent urgently for the town doctor, an old man who had retired to the coast to live out his days in peace. He arrived, already annoyed at yet another interruption as a constant flow of visitors had come to see him since early morning, complaining of thick heads and lethargic limbs. He suspected, rightly, this had been caused by too little sleep and too much drink in the tavern the night before. A sickly hangover from bad beer was probably their most severe aliment: a time-wasting, self-imposed infliction.

An hour later both men were still mad-eyed, raving and clawing at their skins, begging for water to quench their insatiable thirst. What little sense the doctor could make of their collective rants was that their condition was due to the machinations of a sailor who, the night before, had claimed to be able to peel back the fabric of the universe and allow them to peek at their future using Western witchcraft cards.

The old man had left the tavern the night before believing he was destined to meet the final love of his long life that very night and to pursue her at any cost. He had settled on his neighbour's granddaughter, who was barely a quarter of his age and just touching adulthood. After coaxing her to her bedroom window, he yanked her out and took her small, struggling frame to his own home where he repeatedly raped her. He had decided (to his benefit) that her fighting and pleading was a test of his courage and worthiness. Then, he assured himself that her broken submissiveness meant she was finally warming to him, and he now had her heart. When the mob came to drag him away, he believed they were both crying from the threat of lost love.

To his credit, the merchant had come to the quartermaster's office of his own free will. Yet he sounded no less deranged in his musings, and, for a man famed for being so level-headed, this was the most disconcerting factor to the increasingly agitated crowd. It seems that he, too, had talked to the sailor and had found profound knowledge in his cards. He, too, had decided to change his life path from sensible, low risk-investments to high-risk, greater-reward investments. Thus, in half a day, he had gambled away two years of profit on pointless speculation lacking any hint of future gains. He began screaming to all who would listen that the sailor practised some sort of dark art or, at the very least, was in cahoots with those who had just legally robbed him.

The harbourmaster was at a loss, feeling marooned by their scattered ramblings and bipolar behaviours. After examining the two men, the doctor concluded they were suffering from withdrawal symptoms, most likely from poppy plant seeds ground into opium. This, the doctor concluded, would lead to such uncharacteristic behaviour. The question was, where could they have consumed such a concoction? The mob, many who had witnessed the shenanigans in the tavern the night before, knew that would be a good place to begin their search. They started walking back to the tavern, their march for revenge spiced with just a pinch of justice.

By now, word of the fiasco at the harbourmaster's office had reached the sailor, the news leaping from housewife to housewife like a developing pandemic. He hastily dressed, packed his belongings, kissed his latest conquest goodbye and, desperately hoping the mob wouldn't see him, headed for his ship to hide. As he scuttled across the gangplank, he prayed the mob would quickly burn itself out and common sense would be restored.

The mob, finding his room empty apart from a half-conscious girl in the bed, headed to the docks. They found his boat and stormed into the captain's cabin. While terrified and bemused by their tale, he was reluctant to hand the culprit over to them. At the very least, it had to be by legal process involving the proper authority as he could not afford to lose face in front of his crew. Still, he could not hide his eagerness to quickly settle the trouble. His willingness to give up the sailor if backed by the proper authority sent the mob to fetch the harbourmaster.

The sailor had heard all this through the decking cracks. He knew he was cornered and soon would be dead, either legally hung or ripped apart by the mob. But there was no way to flee without being seen. The only way he could escape would be to cause a diversion powerful enough to engulf the whole town's attention, thus sucking out the oxygen of his escapades and making his troubles seem like a minor misdemeanour. In truth, the sailor had been long-sodden by opium abuse that cultivated his own mystic delusions and consumed him as thoroughly as his victim volunteers. Thus, as he made his hasty preparations for escape, he did not realise that the storm had moved and shattered the ship's crates. Still, he had a moment's time to light the slow fuse before the mob dragged him away for judgement.

The mob was halfway to the harbourmaster's office when they heard the explosion. Many mistook it for thunder despite the clear day. Then they realised it was not lightning that lit the sky but salvos of fireworks being transported for celebrations at Hagi. A barrage of artillery struck throughout the town, igniting each of the tiny tinder-dry wooden huts, their small fires mating with the next one. Terrified children ran across rooftops, chased down alleys, the inferno following in their footsteps. The only exit from the blazing hell was up the cliffs, but the way was soon clogged with suffocated corpses now being cremated by the flames. The harbour water turned into torrents from the blast, building into a tsunami that swept up the other ships, smashed them against the piers and demolished the harbour building. There was no escape for the town residents – only the unenviable choice of death by burning or drowning.

From the top of the valley, the sailors who had wandered there earlier watched the town and its people destroyed in an instant. They would never forget the ugly, hot, loud crackle of burning wood and terrified screams before being cut dead by the inferno.

Sakura's great-grandfather was one of those sailors who had watched helplessly from the hillside.

Chapter Thirteen

As I had always discovered when camping, mornings come too bright and early. This morning was no different. The sunlight illuminated our tent like a light box, its gentle morning rays drying out stale sweat. Soon the heat was too much, forcing us to open the flap door to cool down. We climbed out of the tent. Rising from the sea, the sun shimmered on the horizon, reheating the fresh day. In tandem, we munched on our breakfast cereal. I had prepared the scuba diving equipment the night before so we could start as early as possible and not waste a moment of the day. We soon set off, barely giving time for our breakfast to settle or to clear the standard wake-up smog in our heads.

It was less than half an hour down a winding path, sometimes so narrow we had to navigate it sideways. Finally, we reached a small beach half a mile from the dead town. An island to our right bobbed in the distance, a fuzzy blur just far enough away to erase any distinguishing characteristics.

My companion had many talents and graces, but a morning person she was not – one of her few flaws. She had decided to sunbathe while her mind warmed up, leaving me to venture alone. When I asked for direction, she pointed vaguely to the vast expanse of the sea west of the town as if it existed only for our collective private amusement. I studied the shallows for an entry point while absently prepping my breather, checking my mask edges to ensure the seal was watertight, and then tapping my oxygen tank to test for fullness. After strapping it to my back, I hooked up the breather and snapped on my mask. With weight belt in hand, I stepped into the sea. The water first brushed my ankles, then rapidly covered my knees. Moments later, it rippled over my skull, fully conquering my form. It took a few minutes to acclimate myself with the near weightlessness that comes with scuba diving, so I stayed parallel to the shoreline gently skimming beneath the surface. My shadow crawled along the sandy floor, causing crabs to scutter under rocks and fish to scoot in the opposite direction, finally vanishing into the inky depts.

I approached the first cave cut out of the shoreline in less than fifteen minutes. The entrance was shaped like a two-feet-wide mouth with jagged multicoloured coral for teeth, all wrapped in seaweed like ribbons of decay. I kicked my way over to the opening and stared straight into the micro-abyss, a miniature black hole void of light and air. I ran my fingers through the coral's seaweed layers, their slime excretions staining my fingertips. I stayed there, suspended for a moment, my finger ready to click my head torch on to reveal the cave's secrets in a flash of truth. It took a moment for my eyes to adjust, the image before me coming into view like a rapidly developing photograph etching itself into my retinas. I was instantly disappointed to find a shallow and lifeless cave. My light almost reached the back wall, and if I leant forward, I could place my flipper edges at the entrance while brushing my fingertips on the back. There were two other small caves tucked along the shore. Both were as disappointing as the first. When

I remerged from the depths, I found Sakura had changed into a pink bikini so tiny it was almost indecent, so cute I couldn't take my eyes off her. I realised that she could end up being the only stimulating sight of the day, which would definitely be a welcomed bonus to a thus far lacklustre diving expedition.

I spent the next two hours teaching her the basics of scuba diving in a pool filled by a side channel roughly the size and depth of an Olympic-sized pool. The first and most important scuba-diving lessons concern health and safety: never hold your breath as breathing at a steady pace is essential. So *never* hold your breath. Doing that, even for a moment, could rupture your lungs and shatter your brain. Second, when descending, equalise air pressure early and often by holding your nose and gently blowing till your eardrums pop slightly.

The last three lessons were the practical skills necessary for managing basic control in the water. The first: a simple-sounding method on how to clean fog from the face mask by letting in a little water, swishing it round, then draining it out of a corner. In reality, this could take a lifetime to master. The second: clear the regulator to deal with the ironic condition (for divers) of dry-mouth, first by removing the regulator and then sucking a little sea water, using it like mouthwash, before reinserting the regulator and blowing as hard as possible. She found this highly amusing, and her attention span was dwindling. The third: using the buoyancy control device (BCD) to let air in to move up in the water and out to move down. This needed only a short explanation and demonstration. We practised each topic till she was fairly confident, and I was minimally satisfied. As we dashed into the water, I quickly taught her the three essential diving signals for *OK, stop* and *low on air*. By my new student's vacant nod in response, I could tell she was uninterested.

She found the caves to be only fractionally more impressive than I did. She seemed to take to scuba diving as easily as a newly born dolphin to the sea. She was keen to dive together somewhere new for both of us, and with an excited squeal pointed to a rocky outcrop island just offshore. Before giving me a chance to respond positively or negatively, she began skipping rapidly along the shore while I jogged along after her. As we approached, the shoreline changed from a smooth sandy beach to a small, coarse rock face, leaving little enough space for good footholds. The rhythmic slapping of the waves inches below seemed to mock us, challenging us to slip and stumble into their moist embrace.

At times we spread ourselves flat against the rock face, our arms outstretched for balance, our weight all that stopped us from sliding in. An ill-timed breath was all that would be needed to dunk us in. Finally, we arrived at a point opposite the rocky outcrop island offshore. Fate had decided to be kind and rewarded our amateur traverse with a ledge just deep and wide enough for us to prepare for the dive and leave our surplus equipment for us to retrieve later. A few smooth rock outcrops helped with the climb down to the water two feet below. I led and she slid in so close behind that she barely left time for my entrance ripples to subside. Her confidence had grown rapidly, and I hoped that would compensate for her lack of ability. The island was only about a ten-minute swim, even for the most moderate paddler. We swam leisurely through the warm subtropical water; its currents gently pushed us along.

We dived intermittently as we wanted to save our air tanks for the main event but were too curious to let the journey to our destination go by totally unexplored. We weren't disappointed. In the shallows, we saw the fallen pillars and aches of bright stone that had once linked the island outcrop to the mainland.

Eons of gentle current had eroded its foundation. Occasional earthquakes had possibly shattered its carriageway, leaving an undersea home for countless crustaceans, seaweed and eerily transparent jellyfish casually winking at us as they floated by.

When we arrived at the island outcrop, we decided to circumvent it just above the waterline to see if there were any passageways or scramble points to its peak. We were disappointed. There were no easy access points from our position, our already unhelpful bobbing made worse from the slightly stronger sea currents. We returned to our arrival point, the mainland at our backs. I unclicked a small buoy. Its bright-orange dome sat on the water surface like a plastic photosynthetic jellyfish, a six-foot tail extending down under the water. Three bright LEDS attached along the tail flashed at regular intervals, acting as a trail to the surface in case one of us became disoriented or felt in danger. You couldn't miss the flashes – they dazzled so brightly they could be seen from almost all angles.

We dived down together, so close that our limbs intermittently clashed, breaking both our swimming strokes and momentum and causing us to stumble midwater. At about eight feet down, we began circumventing around the island. Our head torches caused schools of neon-glowing fish to flee, speckling the sea like a shimmering rainbow and lighting up the island's rock granite underbelly. As a seasoned diver, I found nothing particularly remarkable about the multicoloured aqua flora and the bounty of life nested within. But my apprentice was obviously thrilled about the new world I had opened to her. Still, I doubt she realised how lucky she was to experience her first scuba dive in such warm splendour and not on a dark afternoon off the bare rock Dover coast – an environment barren of any corral. There, you see only sickly weeds and moss, oxide-bleeding rusted wrecks, and abandoned shopping trolleys as you fight the English Channel's ever-tightening freezing grip.

We had almost completed our first pass when an out-of-place shadow projected by the outer radius of my torch beam caught my attention. It was a round opening, easily enough space to accommodate a medium-sized man like me. Interestingly, it arched upwards and, after closer inspection, into the belly of the island. I signalled for Sakura to wait as I prepared for my ascent. The gap was narrow yet symmetrical, and the scraping on the walls made me wonder if it was man-made. As I took the U-bend up, I was greeted almost instantly with the unmistakable beating of a rippling waterline. With two hard kicks, I pushed off the wall and broke through the water seal, piercing into the vacuum.

The air streaked the outside of my dive mask, instantly blurring my vision and leaving me the impractical task of trying to wipe it with a wet hand. Matters were made worse by the air's coldness, causing condensation to layer over the streaks. I didn't take off my mask as I was concerned that the cave air may have long become toxic. I knew that many a diver had been killed by their eagerness or lack of knowledge in similar circumstances. Or perhaps they just forgot the cardinal law of never removing your breathing gear in such a situation. While the fight for clarity took close to a minute, it seemed much longer, like how a child feels time pass between one Christmas and the next. I paddled forward, my torch lighting up a blur of ground till it unexpectedly faded into shallows. The surprise caused me to slap my flippers and scrape my knees on the jagged rock, slicing them as though with a surgeon's scalpel. A sharp sting to radiated from the fresh wounds from the sea salt.

I stumbled forward, instinctively putting my hands forward to break my fall. Surprisingly, they slammed into solid dry rock. I pulled myself out of the water gently, my temporary blindness finally on the verge of clearing. I sat on the edge, dragging my bloodied knees out the water, still hurting from the rock bites. Then I pulled my legs out. The sting of my wounds faded as the water dripped off my toes. I turned to observe my new surroundings, my sight now three-quarters restored. Now only a faint layer of condensation hindered my investigation. My first quick scan of the nature-made room revealed nothing out the ordinary, just drab grey stone. Until I studied the floor.

The object was blurred, yet it reflected my light distinctly and vividly, like a rare single star in an empty night sky. It looked like a large, well-polished oval stone, centuries of dripping water having worn it to smoothness. I awkwardly wiped my mask free of the last wisps of condensation and picked up the stone, noting its lack of clamminess and surprising weightiness. I was surprised to discover two evenly placed holes just above two tiny triangular cavities in the stone's centre. It finally dawned on me, to my horror, that my fingers were poking through a place where a person's eyeballs once called home. A skull stared back at me with a jawless grin. You would think I would have tossed it away in disgust or shouted out in shocked panic. Instead, I just stood there staring at a skull staring back at me, one studying the other in a moment of illogical absurdity.

I put the skull down, more out of necessity than respect, next to an almost fully toothed jaw I hadn't noticed before. Then, to the right, I saw skeleton body remnants clearly belonging to the skull in fleshier times. The skeleton was sitting in the crossed-legged position in which its owner had taken one final breath. The legs were still in a triangular arc. The arms had fallen to the sides, revealing shallow gaps where muscles and ligaments had long ago rotted away. The ribs had fallen off the ribcage and were scattered around the pelvis. The spine had fallen back, its vertebrae in an uneven line. Strips of rags matted with body decay hung from bones like macabre flags flying in inevitable surrender to doomed fate. On closer inspection, dingy rusted rings encircled the skeleton's ankles and wrists. The rings connected to the outlines of disintegrated chains, their remains now nothing more than rusted-oxide brown stains on the rock floor.

It was clear that the cave's sole occupant had not been there voluntarily. I knew little to nothing of how long it takes for a body to decompose or how the environment assists in body decomposition. The skeleton could be decades young or centuries old – I didn't know. I wondered whether to contact the police or make enquires to the Japanese Archaeologist Society. I was lost in these reflections when I saw a round shadow close by. First, I assumed it was just a rock, but after studying it, I realised it was a large, crumpled ball of fabric of a shaded, slightly muddied brown colour. I picked it up, only to feel an object at the centre, so I unwrapped it to see what secrets it held.

The cloth had two purposes. It had been used as packaging, and it was also a manuscript. I could detect the distinct characters of Japanese kanji letters on it, like mismatched wallpaper patterns of black dye with red outlines. The letters were large and almost childish. They were blurred around the edges, a few lost in such a blur they would be barely readable to a native person, never mind a novice like myself. Given the cave environment, the ink used could only have been the blood of the person who died. I carefully placed the cloth on a nearby dry stone – a luxury in such a damp cave – and gently pulled out the object inside to inspect it in my torchlight.

It was a figure of a fish. As I lifted it closer, its shadow swam across the ground, swallowing its decayed former owner in a single gulp. The figure's smooth face, spiked dorsal fin and long, sloped spine told me it was none other than the King of the Seven Seas: an orca killer whale, something no diver wants to meet, regardless of location or experience. Such a hazard takes place just above the bends and below certain stealth jellyfish, such as the Irukandji, and a few pointed and poisoned puffer fish like the Fugu. At first, I believed the scaled-down killer laying across my palm was carved out of stone. Then, due to its lightness and smooth texture, I deducted that it was crafted out of ivory, probably sea lion or walrus tusk. The bone's halo still radiated through the grime.

I would have continued my inspection, but a shallow gasp and the echo of a body hitting the water behind me shattered my concentration. My companion, out of either curiosity or concern, had followed me. Within seconds after surfacing, Sakura removed her mask, exposing her lungs. Instantly, she succumbed to the toxic stew of fumes which had gathered in the cave over the centuries, choking her with vomit in seconds, felling her with mild convulsions. I quickly replaced her breather. Her lungs gasped in gratitude. I grabbed the orca statue and its gothic wrapping paper, tucking it into my shorts pocket and zipping it shut. Then I speedily scanned the cave with my waterproof camera. When my companion recovered, we hurriedly retreated out of the cave.

She had vomited, a response to fresh air, as soon as we reached the surface after leaving the cave. I had to drag her in the backwards paddling position of a lifeguard, the standard response worldwide to a situation involving an unconscious person. I had been concerned that her condition might deteriorate, a serious occurrence in such a remote location. I would have been at a loss as to how long any help could arrive. Thankfully, she was soon struggling to break free from my grip. About halfway back to the shore, she managed to swim, weakly, her poise and coordination picking up with every passing stroke. I concluded that her symptoms were more from shock then any real ailment.

We returned to camp and she ate heartily – always a good sign – before going to bed early to rest. I hoped the few remaining bruises from falling would lessen, her stomach cramps from vomiting would subside, and by morning she would be ready for our walk back to civilisation. That night in the tent, Sakura slept silently, sweating the final toxins out of her body.

Once she fell asleep, I studied the statue and canvas under the bright moonlight sat in the tent's porch. I had not told her about the find and managed to hide both the statue and the cloth from her. In her fragile state, I doubt she would have noticed or cared anyway. Our adventure complete, the next day we headed for Hagi.

I got home to my flat in Haifuku Kawakami with just a few hours of daylight to spare. Sakura and I had said our goodbyes at the Hagi train station with the standard pleasantries. She had barely mentioned the previous day's alarming episode (at least for me), and when she did, it was mostly overshadowed with embarrassed giggles and heavy sighs. Her little adventure seemed to have barely phased her, leaving few physical effects or psychological traumas. In a few days, I figured she would have placed the ordeal firmly in the past and forgotten it.

Chapter Fourteen

Outside, the rain fell with intensity. A storm had begun a few hours earlier and was still raging. Yet its pounding was mere background noise, barely worth the distraction, and was drowned out by the loudness of the next apartment's television. It assaulted me from all sides, above and below, with a dense, meaningless Japanese barrage. It was vastly irritating. I had resorted to a pair of cheap yet surprisingly effective earplugs. Thankfully, they succeeded in cutting the noise to manageable mummers.

I was hunched over my laptop playing the video I took of the cave walls, the orca statue to the left, the scribbles on the canvas to the right. I had made notes of the written characters, and my first thought was to enter them into the internet search engine for a rough translation. When I did so, I discovered that two-thirds of them didn't seem to exist or, at the very least, had long faded out of fashion. The kanji had been written on the cloth's plain underside. The letters had been etched in one tiny stroke at a time, repeatedly, till the faintest of lines formed. It must have taken hours, maybe days, in pitch dark to do this. It was a testament to the writer's skill and perseverance that the letters were legible at all, definitely an accomplishment almost on a par with the statue that, after gently washing, now gleamed as bright as polished marble. So I was reduced to scattergun internet hopping, looking for appropriate links like a prospector panning for gold. The internet gods would dictate the results, hopefully throwing out tiny nuggets of helpful information from among the deluge of digital dreck.

I soon gave in to these pointless searches. The earplugs were hurting my ears, so I pulled them out. Thankfully, the rain had lessened, so the volume had decreased on the neighbour's television. Only the soft tapping of odd, misplaced raindrops rattled the window. I drank deeply from a glass of water, hoping its coolness would shake my mind into a more constructive search. I now focused on the orca statue. I typed *antiques Japanese tusk statue* in a standard image search and scrolled down the cascade of snapshots. I found some photos from museum archives, often from dim and badly photocopied textbooks. I scrolled down further, scanning each gallery page for a moment till shuffling on.

Progress was slow due to the same photos reappearing on different websites with only slight changes in image resolution. The search results seemed endless, and my mind soon started to drift. I was on the edge of total indifference to the task when my eyes fell on a black-and-white photo. It was not the same as the orca statue in my possession, but it was a close second, maybe its sibling or first cousin. The same immediate family at least. I clicked on the picture to find Japanese text. I ran the site through an online translator just to be presented with mutilated English. The scattering of grammar-stretching punctuation marks and verb tenses was an unfortunate distraction, making even a little enlightenment painfully complex and slow.

The gist of the translation was that the orca statue had not been made by the Japanese but by the Ainu – the native people found only on Hokkaidō. This island is the farthest north of Japan's five main islands. It is also the second largest and least inhabited of the islands. The isolated Ainu people had primarily lived as hunters and fishermen for thousands of years until Emperor Meiji's 1868 victory in the Battle of Toba-Fushimi, which overthrew the Tokugawa Shogunate and established the Meiji Restoration. In 1869, the Restoration established the Hokkaidō Development Commission. The new Japanese government annexed Hokkaidō by forcefully integrating the Ainu into Japanese society. The Development Commission encouraged the *Tondenhei*, former samurai, to settle in Hokkaidō. Because their feudal lords had opposed the Meiji forces, their domains had been abolished, leaving the samurai without gainful employment. Later recruits included thousands of commoners. All came at the expense of the Ainu, who were evicted from the most fertile lands and left only to inhabit the most barren of wildernesses. Ainu customs, such as religious practices, elaborate robes, and full-body tattoos, were outlawed. The Ainu people were forced to use both verbal and written Japanese language. Yet this backfired. Often being hundreds of miles apart on Hokkaidō and isolated from each other, the Ainu people developed dialects unique to each group with verbs and phrases alien to other tribes as well as the common Japanese tongue.

I concluded that this was why I had made so little progress with the canvas. There are literally dozens of different kanji symbols with hundreds of combinations. Without knowing the Ainu people who had written these words, or at least the area where the canvas came from, there was little hope of ever deciphering the letters without additional research or, more realistically, consulting an expert. And being so far south, there were no experts nearby.

The only conclusion I could come to from the scant available evidence was that the corpse might be the prophesying pyromaniac whose actions had burned Inaka to the ground almost two centuries ago. The legend said that he had hailed from the shores of Hokkaidō – the Ainu heartland – and if he had been chained and left to starve to death, that seemed a suitable method of revenge for the total incineration of a village.

Realising this, I went to bed as the new school term started in the morning. Even though I had hit a brick wall, I hoped that with enough time, research and perseverance combing the internet, I could mine some nuggets of useful information from the terabytes of slag.

***

It was the last school term of the academic year. Thankfully, we were drawing ever closer to summer break. Yet my free time was sacrificed each week because I had to help with last-minute cram sessions. The time I could devote to my cave project research was mostly confined to weekends, afternoons and the odd empty evening when my brain was not too burned out from hammering English verbs and punctuation into children's heads six hours straight each weekday.

During the final week of the term, my temporary peers evaluated my teaching skills. To my surprise, they found my work to be way beyond satisfactory, and I was judged to be one of the all-round best they had ever had – a true credit to the JET programme and my country. Whether all this praise was genuine or just kindness is anyone's guess.

On the last day, my class presented me with a thank-you card and handmade gifts they had made in secret in their own time. Despite their limited concentration in class, these gifts and their tearful goodbyes touched me.

Finally free of teaching duties, I focused on the mystery of my recent Ainu artefact treasures. My research taught me much general information about the Ainu people and their history and customs, especially concerning animal and human polytheism. But I was shut out of most the discussion because it was written solely in Japanese. So I was condemned to beginner guides and the odd English website that recycled the same information over and over again. I soon had to admit defeat and started to look for a local expert to help, only to find that the nearest one was in Tokyo, half a day away by train. As I was planning to spend a few weeks of my summer break there anyway, this was hardly a massive inconvenience. I had hoped to get my friend Johnny to help me as a guide, but he had not replied to my last email despite prompt replies each time I had contacted him before. I put this down to his earlier break-up from school and thus having too much of a good time.

I soon set off for Tokyo, the cave objects in my bag and a printout of Johnny's email address in my coat pocket. I hoped to meet up with him anyway. At last, I was beginning a journey that might unravel this curious Japanese mystery.

Part Two

Chapter Fifteen

I had caught the earliest train I could afford, which left Shin-Yamaguchi Station in late morning. I had spent the previous day getting my affairs for the next academic year in order and managed to secure another year as an English teacher at the same school but with older pupils. This meant I got to keep the same apartment, so I didn't have to lug my whole expat life around with me in the interim – just the bare travelling essentials. I had said my goodbyes for the summer to my neighbours and made sure my landlord knew I would be returning in six weeks by paying two months' rent upfront. Tenants' rights in Japan are almost medieval, and they are even worse for a foreigner.

The day was light and breezy. While the full throbbing heat of summer had not yet arrived in the southern Yamaguchi Prefecture, I knew that had been true for Tokyo for weeks, evaporating energy, cramping limbs and dehydrating minds. I knew from gossip that Tokyo summers are notoriously hot where the streets catch the heat and wrap it around the metropolis like an electric blanket. I had prepared my wardrobe for this assault the best I could.

I found my seat on the train, stashed my suitcase, and the train started. The landscape flew by like a slide show carousel.

Nature was in full bloom now, unlike the autumn melancholy I had observed when I last travelled this route. The towns that had looked deserted when I passed last autumn were now a mass of motion, reminding me of a kicked-down ant hill. The paddy fields had layers of rice as far as the eye could see, swaying and shimmering with just the whisper of wind. I was enjoying my trip more than last time; not surprising as my previous apprehension was absent. Now, I was heading towards a friendly face as opposed to galloping into the unknown.

I entered Tokyo in the early evening. The city's lights had not dimmed by even the faintest wisp of a watt in my twelve-month absence. If anything, my exile now made their gleam seem even brighter. The train pulled into the deceivingly cool Shinjuku Station. I was again flanked by escalators and crowds of people so dense that moving was almost impossible at any reasonable speed. I had decided to spend my first two nights in a hotel to get my bearings. It was now late afternoon and trying to find Johnny in the largest metropolitan city on earth with little info to his whereabouts – and while travel-weary – was an experience that I could do without.

There is a perception by some in the West that Japan is ninety-nine per cent temples and one per cent sand gardens inhabited by women wearing over-decorated silk dressing gowns and restaurants selling only raw fish. This is the same logic that says a castle crowns every English hill and buffaloes still patrol the American Great Plains sprinkled with tepees. Those who think this are obviously idiots. The sad fact is that Tokyo is primarily made of concrete, earthquake-proof structures and eateries, which are often the type of fast-food chains found worldwide.

I had chosen to stay at the Shin Okubo Sekitei Hotel Tokyo, a basic business model. This unassuming hotel was definitely quaint and out of the way. The hidden back-alley entrance was so narrow that two people could barely pass each other without bumping shoulders. It was hard for Japanese people to find, never mind illiterate foreigners like me. The hotel website had three pictures, including directions, with a slide for each stage of the epic journey. They presented it as if the golden city El Dorado was at the end of the trail, and not just a simple bedroom. To get there, you first had to traverse a large zebra crossing straight out of the Shin-Okubo Station. Thankfully, the station had only one exit. Outside, I turned left and walked through Ōkubo, the ethnic enclave of Tokyo's Korea Town, before making a sharp turn by a supermarket to arrive at the hotel. The front of the hotel was whitewashed with a short skirt of grey at street level. Four pale green, heat-exhausted plants, sulking in pots along the wall, provided the only colour. Two alloy bins flanked the hotel's doorway, and but for a small, in-your-face billboard announcing the hotel's name, the building could have easily been mistaken for a modest house.

Upon entering, I was given the red-carpet treatment, the entrance hallway's carpet as crimson and spotless as that used for the Oscars. I booked in with my best broken Japanese to replies in shattered English. After mutually heartfelt bows, I headed up the stairs to my first-floor room, passing a tourist brochure stand with books written in every major language of the globe. The wooden stairs gave way to a slate-lined floor. Knee-high jagged rocks set in a thin layer of gravel shadowed the banister. A single miniature cherry blossom tree (possibly of the plastic variety) was the only splash of colour against the grey walls. Three proud bamboo poles stretched from slate floor to ceiling like wooden Roman columns by my room door.

The air conditioning in my room was thankfully at full throttle, the window a thin vale against the pulsing heat. After

I unpacked and freshened up in the smallest shower on earth, it was time to find something to fill my belly, then take an early night for a sharp start in the morning.

Outside, neon-signs' radiance grew by the moment as night replaced the daylight's few remaining embers. My hotel was in Shinjuku, one of Tokyo's twenty-three special wards, which has many attractions but only a few cultural delights. It also has one of the busiest train stations in the world, which I had escaped earlier that day. Shinjuku is also home to Tokyo's famous Kabukichō entertainment district, by all accounts the largest red-light district in the world. I had no interest in that sort of action tonight as it would require staying up till dawn to fully benefit such shenanigans, and I wanted to be asleep early. I walked over the Shinjuku Station bridge, vibrating with trains skimming underneath. An army of buskers lined each side, strumming their guitars while singing everything from the newest Japanese chart hits to Bob Dylan in bad overtones driven by their own competing passions. It was all a din to my ears. I dove down a side street and strode into the nearest half-empty restaurant with an English menu.

The Kindenmaru Shibuya Dogenzaka Ramen shop is nestled between a shoe store and a cake shop. A person-sized billboard was propped next to the doorway advertising its wares of noodles or pork and eggs showered in a variety of sauces and nestled in a rainbow of vegetables. My head brushed past the customary red cloth banner tassels rimming the gold spray-painted sign to find a prepared meal vending machine. Large, coloured photos of dishes made understanding Japanese unnecessary. After I fumbled in some coins, the vending machine duly spat out an order ticket, saving me the embarrassing aggravation of trying to order from the red-hatted chefs in bad Japanese. That left them to focus their attention on preparing the meals in an organic production line over the thunder of the clattering of pans and hissing of boiling water.

The noodles stewed merrily in their bowl. One thing I learnt soon after arriving in Japan: it was always best to let the noodles settle for about thirty seconds to let the ingredients and stock merge and be absorbed into the dough pores as they gently twirl and convulse in the heat. I sipped from my glass of ice-cold water, watching the rising steam from the bowl, then instantly misting and condensing on the sides, drops streaking down and dripping on the table. The outside breeze pulsed through the doorway. The restaurant was emptier than I thought it would be when I first entered. The congested street outside had deceived me. I put this down to the fact that it was the twilight hour when people were either preparing to eat at home with their families or readying themselves to go out with their friends for the night. There was a stillness begging to unfold in the night air.

While Johnny had not replied to my last two emails, I had managed to get his mobile number from the JET course HQ after sweet-talking an assistant. Data protection evidently is not as big an issue in Japan as it is in the West. I tapped the number into my mobile, a small pay-as-you-go affair, and I sent the most basic of all greeting messages to Johnny:

Hi its Mike from JET. I'm in Tokyo for a few days do you want to meet up?

The message disappeared with the signature bleep, and I started to slurp my noodles with the unnatural rhythm of a foreigner.

The bowl was almost empty with only a few small stragglers left, so small they would barely feed the tiny gnat I found drowning in the cooling broth, when my phone beeped, signalling a message arrival. Since I had just texted Johnny, I was not surprised by the sender and was pleased he had replied so quickly. I had begun to wonder if some unfortunate circumstance had befallen him. His message was plain:

Hi mate I live in Higashisuna area in Koto-ku district now. We can meet up tomorrow around 6:00p.m. at the Caffe Topos. See you then.

I read the message over a few times and mulled it over in my mind. After asking the waitress, who spoke surprisingly good English, where the Higashisuna area was, she informed me that it was deep in the suburbs, almost at the edge of the city limits and just over an hour by train from my present point. I tipped her with a wink, and she skipped away to her next customer. I found it strange that Johnny had moved to such a remote part of the city, unless that was where his next placement was, and he was getting ready to settle in for next term. Yet I had a nagging feeling in the back of my mind that something was amiss that I couldn't shake. By the time I had readied myself for bed, that apprehension had almost disappeared. I planned to visit the Ainu Museum at the University of Tokyo in the morning, then Johnny in the evening, so I went to sleep with the knowledge that tomorrow was planned out.

Chapter Sixteen

I rose early, washed quickly, ate sparingly and left the hotel promptly. I wanted to arrive at the museum early, ready for when it opened its doors at 10:00a.m. I hoped it would be easier to catch a curator with a morning spring in their step and eager to educate than in the late afternoon when they would be tired after the novelty of the day had worn off.

After a brief thirty-minute train journey, I encamped outside a coffee shop – the Café Bon Art – with the museum's front gate in my view. I didn't want to seem too eager, so I decided to wait till around 10:15a.m. to enter the museum, giving me time to gauge the foot traffic and weigh the size of the crowd I would be dealing with. I soon learnt that the Café Bon Art had a lazy vibe in the morning and afternoon. It was frequented mostly by students, but at night, some of Tokyo's top classical musicians, from novice pianists to veteran violinists, played for local connoisseurs at the café. This place had a traditional Japanese rock garden and pond, and tree saplings behind glass against the back wall of two-tone browns. The Hongo Antique Gallery on the floor above added to the chic artistic ambiance.

The Ainu Museum is found in the imaginatively named The University Museum, The University of Tokyo (UMUT for short). It was a modest medium-size building of grey concrete and fake wooden panelling, an off-shoot to Tokyo University's main south campus. UMUT was ringed by an iron fence and graced an unassuming neighbourhood with a scattering of mismatched trees for gardens and haphazardly placed stores – from a yoga studio to a recycling centre. Compared to the gothic splendour of the University of Cambridge, the spires of the University of Oxford, or the regal excesses of the British Museum, UMUT seemed rather quaint and tame. According to the website, UMUT was maintained mostly by volunteers and student staff. I got the impression that most of its patrons were bored children on school trips or university students researching their final thesis. I didn't want to be swamped in a sea of sailor uniforms or have to wait too long walking behind a queue of wannabe academics. I finally entered the museum around 10:30a.m. The entrance queue had evaporated in less than five minutes after opening, and as there seemed to be no mad rush to enter, so I decided in was safe to slip in.

To get to the Department of Archaeology I first had to make my way past the Department of Nature. A horse, sheep, and flock of chickens and cockerels greeted me. All were badly stuffed by substandard taxidermy. It was all a bit gothic, but the next room turned up the macabre factor to eleven. Wooden cases were neatly stacked from floor to ceiling along all four of the twenty-feet high walls. Each case contained from a few to a dozen species of insects, their limbs pinned spread-eagled in timeless slumber, ready to be examined. Radiant butterflies in riotous shades of nature rested next to gargoyle moths, their vileness hidden within their hoods. There were squadrons of massive scarab beetles, their spread wings hovering in interrupted immortal flight. Every example of nature's endless wonders was there, from scorpions of the vast desert planes to spiders of the dense rain forests. All were organised in regimented lines, encased in eternity, windowed air-tight tombs. Museum spectators stared inquisitively, moving from box to box. One day, their fates would be similar, but they would be buried in boxes and forgotten, their lives too inconsequential to be worth displaying on a wall.

I finally arrived at the Department of Archaeology after wading through the Department of Nature's exotic creatures crucified to their box walls. The room was square with a small garden in the middle. It was much quieter than the bustle I had just left. The Ainu exhibits were arranged chronologically, so I could follow a path from the right, starting at the end of the last Ice Age 25,000 years ago when hunter-gathering was the only game in town, and ending at the turn of the previous century, around 1899, when their assimilation was almost complete with the Law for the Protection of Native Hokkaidō Aborigines. This Law and its associated policies were designed to fully integrate the Ainu into Japanese society and erase the Ainu culture and identity. I hastily scanned the first eras, reading only the basic bullet points of each display as I was only slightly interested in the periods when Neanderthals thrived, as 40,000-year-old information was unlikely to be of use for my present endeavour. I moved forward, ventured around the corner, and found the eighth-century displays showing when the Ainu mastered farming basics and hut building. I found that impressive since their climate mimicked a mild Ice Age two-thirds of the year. Finally, I came upon a display of Ainu crafts, beginning with basic pottery and coarse jewellery. I carefully scanned each item, noticing how their skills and methods grew in complexity and craftsmanship over thousands of years.

I had not brought the statue or canvas with me because I feared being accused of thievery. I had no clue about Japanese law concerning found treasure, and I didn't want to have to explain how I found them in a decomposed shrivelled shrine of human remains. I had taken a few photos of everything, which I printed so as to compare the items with similar ones that might be in the museum family. I was stunned to find a black-and-white photograph almost identical to my own colour photo of the statue, faded with age. It was almost 150 years old. I read the display case banner – *Lost treasure of the Ainu* – a dry and lifeless title, but the tale written underneath was thrilling in the extreme.

Apparently, it was the winter of 1869 when the forced integration policy neared its most destructive height. This was when unique Ainu cultural treasures such as the centuries-old two-headed musical stringed instruments and multicoloured, lavishly woven robes were stolen, or "forcefully bought" (depending on which side tells the tale), by a Japanese lord, Oguri Tadamasa. Emperor Meiji had sent him to civilise the scattered Ainu tribes around Hokkaidō Island. The Ainu treasures were then transported around the country for two years until mid-1871 with the more traditional treasures of jade statues and gold idols of the recently fallen Tokugawa Shogun. They were shown in places from rural town halls to the Emperor's Imperial Palace to prove the Meiji Restoration's invincibility. Early in the tour, grainy photographs were taken, and documentation was made. At the end of the tour, the group was to return to Oguri Tadamasa on the most northern island, Hokkaidō. However, once the group reached Hokkaidō, it was ambushed on a forest path by a handful of Ainu rebels, their robes and beards streaming in the wind, the last true patriots who refused to be stripped of their dignity. The Ainu attackers massacred the tour managers and their guards and took back the treasures that had been stolen from them with the gold and jade statues of the fallen Tokugawa Shogun as a bonus. A massive hunt commenced in the surrounding Ainu villages and towns, but not a trace could be found of the stolen treasures. There were no surviving witnesses to describe the assailants, who were suspected of disappearing deep into the far northern Hokkaidō mountains, an isolated region outside the control of Japanese law. The trail grew cold and the treasures – including those like the orca statue I had found – were lost to time. The episode eventually became known as the Tokugawa Treasure, one of Japan's almost-forgotten mysteries.

I was lost in concentration, holding my own photo of the statue next to the display case, when I felt a presence behind me. The dim reflection in the glass display case confirmed that I was being observed. Realising that hiding the photo would heighten my watcher's suspicion, I simply turned to face my stalker.

It was a young Japanese woman. She looked about my age, maybe a shade younger, her blush of youth hidden under a thin layer of make-up. She wore a very practical black pant suit and white blouse. A small plastic name badge sat cheekily on the right side of her jacket, unfortunately in Japanese. I gathered this was her work outfit. Her eyes darted from mine to the photo I was holding, which she seemed vastly more interested in, before she returned her gaze to mine. I knew I should introduce myself, but I didn't know if she spoke English and was embarrassed to use my elementary Japanese.

'Hello, do you need any assistance?'

Her English was way above average, her pronunciation almost perfect. I was taken aback, having anticipated an awkward exchange of broken English and badly pronounced Japanese. Her raised eyebrows acknowledged she had seen my surprise.

After a moment of stunned silence, I remembered how to form my words and that she had asked a question meriting a response.

'Yes, I was wondering if you could tell me anything more about this display?'

Her eyes brows lifted slightly. Peaking over the rims of her glasses, she approached the display while keeping one eye pinned on my photo.

'There are no more major details to tell, really, just a few minor ones. After the assault, the Meiji Restoration spent the whole of 1870 in Hokkaidō searching for the Ainu rebels and the stolen treasures – right up until the heavy winter snows made searching impossible. There were plans to resume after the following spring's thaw, but a number of nationwide uprisings lead by the remnants of the Tokugawa Shogunate against the Meiji Restoration broke out in the new year, and most able-bodied men were conscripted to fight elsewhere. The story, suppressed as an embarrassing imperial defeat by a gang of beggar bandits, was forgotten till after World War II. It was eventually rediscovered by Nakajima Kurando after the loosening of censorship laws during the Allied occupation. Today, armchair archaeologists, enticed by the mystery, continue the search for the lost treasure, but to no avail. It did not help that as revenge for the assault, Imperial Japan targeted the Ainu tribes living close to the assault, scattering and sometimes forcefully relocating them to other parts of Hokkaidō. Apart from misguided conspiracy theories in internet chat rooms, this treasure hunt has been thoroughly unsuccessful. I'm curious, where did you get that photo?'

'I printed it off the internet as reference,' I replied, trying to sound sincere and confident in my tone.

'Impressive, seeing as colour photography was not invented until at least fifty years after the exhibition, hence why all the pictures are in plain black and white.'

She left the accusation hanging in the air between us. Her expression reeked of insult and a hint of pity for me, the incompetent perpetrator.

'What are the odds?' I said, so embarrassed I could barely breathe. She smirked, curling her lips, a quick flick of her tongue polishing her pink lip gloss.

'If you should remember anything else about the photograph and how you came about it, please contact me.'

She handed me a business card in both Japanese and English. I slid it meekly into to my wallet as she briskly walked away to another visitor. I left shortly after, making sure I had not been followed. Even though the encounter had been brief, she came across as the observant type and I did not want her following me. I feared she could easily unravel the truth from my poor web of lies before tattling on me to the authorities. Finally, alone on the small train platform headed to the Higashisuna area suburbs in the Koto-ku district to meet Johnny, I realised my paranoia was unjustified.

Chapter Seventeen

I stepped off the train at Minami-Sunamachi Station. Like a small concrete mouth, it regurgitated me into the outside edge of Higashisuna just before 5:00p.m. The neighbourhood sat on one bank of the Arakawa River, where the Tokyo city frontier ends. Just over the river, the rest of Japan officially begins.

I explored the general area, dodging down back streets and scuttling down side alleys, and finally arrived at our meeting place, Caffe Topos. It was hidden between man-made canyons of concrete layered with flaking paint. I was early and decided to kill some time with a stroll by the nearby riverbank. The area was heavily industrialised and dirty from spewing chimneys and rippling lorry fumes. It was soon apparent why the riverside was so popular. The smog-breeding concrete towers of the workhouses and the resident flats were depressing and hot. This slim barrier of green creeping by the river's edge, doubling as a flood barrier, was a tranquil harbour from the croaking of window air conditioners and screeching of traffic-jammed cars.

Eventually, I walked back and entered Caffe Topos. I sat by the window and waited for Johnny to arrive. The bouncy, sunny interior was the polar opposite of the stale, grey Tokyo suburbs just beyond the window. I ordered a light green tea and slowly sipped it while I flipped the museum curator's business card between my fingers. Flicking it from one knuckle to the next, I contemplated contacting her. Otherwise, my investigation would be at a premature end. If nothing else, I might become a minor national hero if I found and returned a lost relic. Nothing is more of an aphrodisiac than being a hero. I thought of her slim body. Her flirty nature could develop into something else, which might be a reward in more ways than one.

Thinking of her, I was day-dreaming my way through various karma positions, just getting her out of her underwear, when Johnny arrived and snapped me back to reality. He sat opposite me, quiet. I assumed the rigmarole of Tokyo life with its twenty-five-hour waking days had rung the life out of him. His slouched position seemed to be a testament to his tiredness. He fidgeted with his hands, repeatedly stroking and bending each finger, only ceasing when his drink arrived. He grabbed it with his right hand, leaving his left lonely and morose. It was a character trait I had not noticed on our first meeting. I asked him the standard set of questions one does when greeting a mild acquaintance not seen for a while. He avoided giving any real answers other than yes or no. Johnny had definitely lost his former chirpiness. His once-bright eyes now regarded me from a hollow gaze. It was as though something had killed his former aura. Or maybe he was just suffering from an extreme hedonistic hangover. Or culture shock had burned out his last brain fuse.

Seeing his unwillingness to talk about how he was doing, I decided to tell him about my adventures down south. He was uninterested till I mentioned the orca tusk statue and the cloth script. That perked his interest, and he became intently curious. I finished my story with an account of the morning meet up with the museum's curvy curator.

'Can I see the photos?'

He mustered more enthusiasm in those five words than he had during my whole half-hour monologue. I pushed the photos across the table, and he studied it intensely as though simultaneously seeing his salvation and personal abyss.

'Can I keep these?' he demanded, more than asked, while sliding them into his pocket. A slight shrug of my shoulder was my only hint of protest.

At that point, he began to open up and enlighten me about his time in Tokyo. Still, it seemed like a thin performance forced through grated teeth, as though awarding me for the photo. My overall impression from the few details he offered was that his experience had, on the whole, been unfulfilling and depressing. His expectations for fun and games had been deflated by having to work from nine to five. The hour was soon up. Before he left, Johnny asked me one final question.

'Do you intend to ring this woman?'

'Yes, tonight. I will try to arrange a meeting tomorrow as she seems keen to continue her enquiries.'

'Text me straight after. I'd like to know how it goes.'

Johnny left me sitting at the table as he departed through the door. I noticed that his eyes had not left the wall clock since he had entered. Clearly, something was bothering him. The pressure of time forcefully pushing him on – but to where, why and by whom? I was at a loss and had no chance to enquire.

Chapter Eighteen

I left Caffe Topos to face rush hour commuters, all returning home to reclaim the only part of the day which they truly owned. When I finally got to my hotel, I was exhausted. I ate an unremarkably presented and bland dinner in the hotel cafeteria, then returned to my room.

I laid down on my bed. It was too early to sleep yet too late to do anything constructive. Seeing that it was not yet past 8:00p.m., I decided to text the curator. First, though, I resolved to do a little cyber research on her name, "Chihiro". As with all Japanese names, the full meaning depended on the second kanji. The first kanji always meant the same – thousand. The second kanji could mean "fathoms" or "abundance", but in this case, it meant "gains". Next, I did a pinch of internet stalking to find out the basics of Ms Chihiro's life. I began at the Tokyo University Department of Archaeology internet site. I ran it through a third-party translation website and discovered that she was twenty-two years old, in her final year of university scholarship, and working on the final draft of her dissertation. A glance at her social media accounts showed she was from the village of Ueno in the rural district of the Gunma Prefecture, just out of Tokyo's grasp. The place looked as action-packed and exciting as my very own Haifuku Kawakami down south. She had the few obligatory photos taken with friends atop an unassuming hill outside Ueno, a couple with classmates at the university, and finally some standard scenery shots of her hometown and Tokyo city life. Given her looks, I was surprised to learn she was single.

I thought about the best way to open the dialogue. It occurred to me that if I spent as much time and dedication on the more important aspects of my life, many things might be different in a vastly more positive way. Text messages are unique because audio, allowing one to judge intent, is absent. Body language, perhaps revealing hidden Machiavellian notions, is also absent. Texting offers crisp words, nothing more. I decided on honesty over deceitfulness as I had already insulted her intelligence. I needed to start again. I would open with a compliment on her knowledge and expertise. It couldn't be too obviously flattering – there's definitely a fine line between endearing and creepy. I would finish with a veiled plea for her help to let her know she was needed. I mapped out sentences for my text's beginning, middle and end points, and after a final glance for punctuation, I clicked send. I left her response to blind fate as I had no clue as to her mood or whether she would have the time or inclination to help me an inch.

Her rather quick reply was disappointingly sterile. She said she'd meet me at the Cafe Kingyo-zaka, near her university dorm, surprisingly early the next day. To meet her, I would have to be awake and ready at the coattails of dawn. With that thought, I rolled over to sleep, confused by Johnny's recent insincerity and excited about the meeting with "her majesty" the next morning.

Somehow, I managed to wake up and drag myself to the café. While only three subway stops away, it was buried in a maze of back alleys, which would have put the minotaur's labyrinth of Crete to shame. I was still only half awake and exhausted from the rush of getting there on time, a situation brought about more by luck than skill. I only had a few fragile moments to compose myself when she arrived. I hoped that by the end we would both be singing the same song.

Quaint was not cute enough to describe Cafe Kingyozaka. A bright red and very large wooden fish hung outside, proudly displaying the shop's 350 years as one of Tokyo's prime goldfish shops before branching out into the coffee and cake crowd thirteen years ago with the Goldfish slash restaurant. This Cypriniformes store had been in the same family for seven generations. Children fished for goldfish in the outside tanks, their parents watching while eating lunch. In the wood-panelled room where I sat waiting for Chihiro, every table was paired with a large ash tray – a long-forgotten relic in Europe. A scattergun array of whimsical pictures littered the walls, from small, elegant frames of delicate poppies to proud, black birds standing at attention. The opposite wall was filled with disparate chipboard frames, a spectrum of mismatched oddities hanging there in unkept glory.

Chihiro entered, arriving like clockwork, as though she alone had the privilege of commanding the movement of time itself. She was wearing a simple sleeveless dress that ended just an inch above the knee. The neckline dipped with a sharp V to no more than a centimetre above the valley of her moderate cleavage. By the other admiring glances of the other male caffeine addicts there, I noticed they, too, found her intensely attractive. The waitress, casually familiar with Chihiro, took her order as soon as she sat down. Her tea arrived momentarily. She sipped it, placed the cup back on its saucer, then laced her fingers around the cup and looked up straight at me.

'Good morning, and what a beautiful morning it is!' I had decided that a wide, clear statement would be best to ease into the conversation.

'A typical Tokyo summer day must be dull for you, as I hear the weather in England can change from one moment to the next without reason or warning. We don't have such a variety in our seasons here.'

It was a strange and over-complex way to open a conversation. Was I missing some sly metaphor which had become lost in translation? I decided to end the awkward silence that had slinked in after her last statement by producing the orca statue and inscribed cloth. I checked to see if anyone else in the room was watching, but no one seemed even vaguely interested.

She picked up the statue in her delicate hand and studied it meticulously for almost a full minute before gingerly placing it down. She then studied the canvas. Frustration graced her face momentarily before she regained her composure. She dumped it next to the statue as if it was a common rag.

'As your Western saying goes, I have both good news and bad news. The good news is the statue is authentic and the canvas seems to give directions to the statue's other siblings. The bad news is I can only vaguely translate the kanji on the canvas. I do know an expert in Sapporo – the only one possible, I may add – who could fully decipher the clues.'

As she said this, I slowly inched my hand forward to take the artefacts back. They were almost in my grasp when her hand came down on top of mine, bringing my pull to a standstill.

'I have a proposition. We both travel to Sapporo to see the professor and from there to wherever the inquiry may lead us. If we find the rest, we'll bring them back to the museum. You will be famous and rewarded, no doubt, and I can use the story in my final university thesis. That will give me the choice of internships anywhere in the world.'

She released my hand. I picked up the artefacts and replaced both in my bag. I was already chomping at the bit.

'When do we leave?' I asked before considering any consequences.

'Tomorrow, early morning. I will make the arrangements. We'll travel by train. I can get a student discount for both of us. I'll text you the details later.'

She sprang out her seat, pecked me on the cheek, and galloped out the coffee shop as fast as she could. The stern woman who had entered shortly before had been replaced by the giddy girl who was just leaving, yet in the glass door reflection, I could swear her smile fell back into a sterile slate the moment she believed I could no longer see her face. I put this down to possible ill-refracted light or mild paranoia. I returned to my hotel to drop off the artefacts before meeting Johnny. In my excitement, I had almost forgotten about him.

Chapter Nineteen

I got off the metro at Nihon-Odori Station in the Kanagawa Prefecture as Johnny had told me to do for today's meet up. The station was almost deserted, as rare a phenomenon in Tokyo as a dry winter day in London. The station was the second-to-last stop on the line. My travel time was the rare space between lunch and clocking off, probably the reason for the unusual lull of people. As soon as I left the station, I was struck by the heavy industrial landscape around me. It was clear that I was in one of Tokyo's manufacturing centres. National brand loyalty and extra-high import taxes and tariffs kept Tokyo's industry strong. The corporate headquarters of Japan's first mass-market radio maker, Pioneer, called this area home along with car manufacturing giant Nissan and dozens of other companies. The area was also home to a splattering of cultural sites, the most famous being the traditional quaint pastels of the Yokohama Doll Museum. Its occupants were from dynasties stretching from Yokohama's founding to modern times. There was also the factory metallic of the ultra-futuristic Gundam Factory, a shrine devoted to the TV series about robotic battle suits fighting epic wars among the stars.

Johnny had said he would meet me at the station. Right on cue, he appeared out of a back alley, hurry written in his footsteps and worry lining his face. The bar he had told me about was not too far, and soon he was leading me on a fast walk through side streets and alleyways, which I had now come to expect in any commute around Tokyo. The alleyways were so narrow I could have stretched out my arms and reached side to side with no problem. The tall factory walls meant that even in mid-afternoon their shadows blocked the sunlight. The paths were full of litter bred by poverty like a man-made fungus.

Johnny said that the bar we were going to doubled as the prize exchange for the Pachinko parlour next door. Pachinko is like vertical pinball crossed with a normal arcade machine. The goal is to collect as many ball bearings as possible to exchange for currency. They are often based on anime or video game franchises, and their popularity is so vast that venues can hold hundreds, even thousands, of gamblers. Hunched over together, like a canopy, they watch their money bounce and rattle away for an easy win before inevitably, like so much in life, falling deep into the oblivion of a losing streak. In the end, they leave the machine's bright flashing siren lights and encouraging cat calls to begrudgingly return to the humdrum of reality. Pachinko is Japan's personal gambling addiction, an epidemic effecting almost four per cent of the population.

Nearly all forms of gambling are illegal in Japan, but Pachinko offers a legal loophole where winning prize tokens can be legally "sold" for cash at a separate vendor located off-premises. These vendors, independent from but often owned by the Pachinko parlour owner, then sell the tokens back to the parlour at the same price paid for them, plus a small commission. Thus, they turn a cash profit without technically violating the law. What a perfect satire on capitalism. The shouts of glee in Pachinko parlours are as deafening as those heard on Wall Street trader floors, the scrolling video screens as seductive as the Dow Jones Index.

At last, we found the bar next to 123 Pachinko. 123 Pachinko proudly dominated the area, the bar meekly cowering in its shade, a slip of red, flickering neon the only indication of life. Beside the Pachinko parlour, the bar was a dim affair. Table lamps flickered like small cries for help. A thick cloud of cigarette smoke filled every gloomy corner. The room appeared deserted with no bartender guarding the bar or glass collector waiting to pounce. The only occupant was a large man sitting at a single table in the centre of the room as though in his private universe. He was well dressed for such a bar. There were two other seats at his table, and Johnny urged me to sit in one while he took the other. As we sat down, the man leant forward, his garish suit reflecting the table light. He wore a bright, neon-purple jacket over a sky-blue shirt, an assemblage that even the most aggressively attention-seeking teenage girl would be ashamed to wear. I was now ninety per cent sure this was no ordinary bar and the man opposite me was anything but a simple landlord.

I had seen members of the Japanese yakuza – a semi-legal mafia, for all intents and purposes – in Hagi, close to my home in the south. Their dead giveaway neon suits and fully tattooed bodies were admired worldwide by others of that disposition. Unlike their Western counterparts, everyone knows who the yakuza are. They even have their own business offices and fan magazines. Yet Japan, debatably the most sensible country on earth, has an organised crime network with more members than the rest of the world's crime families combined. The largest clan – the Yamaguchi-gumi – is twice the size of all other world's crime families combined. There are over 1,000 clans sprinkled over the islands. The public tolerates them, perhaps out of some sense of inherited feudal loyalty. With his gold-ringed fingers flickering like comets, the man motioned me to sit, indicating a firm order, not a casual invitation. As I sat down, two large shadows loomed over Johnny and me. I turned to find two burly stone-faced men with a look of heavy violent intent etched in their scarred faces. My host smiled, possibly the only honest aspect of this whole situation. That worried me the most.

'Hello,' he said coldly. 'Johnny, tell me much about you.'

Though he mentioned Johnny, our host's attention was solely fixed on me. His English was unpolished yet adequate enough to carry a conversation. He didn't wait for a verbal response, just my frown acknowledging that I understood him.

'He say you find very interesting something near Hagi that can kill some of his big debt with us,' he said with menace in his voice.

Out of the corner of my eye, I saw Johnny grimace with a mixture of shame, regret and fear. Yet again, my host didn't require an answer. The anxiety flickering across my face was enough for him to see that I understood the weight of the situation.

'So we take your statue and give you this one.' With a sinister gaze, he lifted up a bad replica. 'You keep as souvenir. This is strong request. Not negotiation. Understand? But your statue only pays back to us some of his sin debt.'

Weighed down by his ugly threat, I nodded as graciously as possible and unsteadily picked up the replacement statue, turning and studying it at arm's length. I was, of course, stalling for time. I knew if I tried to escape by running, I would not make it halfway to the door, and if by some miracle I did, I'd soon be tracked down within minutes. A fleeing white man was only slightly less rare in these parts than a unicorn in England. I wouldn't be able fight my way out. I would be floored in seconds – even when the odds are equal, physical combat was hardly my forte. The most pressing fact of all was that if something bad happened, no one knew where I was. How much time would pass before someone would begin to look for me? By the time anyone missed me, I would be long dead and buried. Negotiation was the only option open to me. Even if I fully cooperated and gave them what they wanted, I knew I would probably end up with the same dead-end result. Once they had the statue, Johnny and I would be toast.

'I have a counteroffer.'

Johnny stared at the floor and started nervously rocking in his seat. His hands held each side of his shaking head, his abject fear visible to everyone. My host looked at me coldly. Yet as I told him my plan to go to the north with an expert to find more treasure, his coldness thawed into a small smile of anticipation. A bit of saliva from the edge of his lips and the sly movement of eyes revealed his greed. I was careful not to mention Chihiro's name and indicated that I only had a vague idea which city in Hokkaidō we would be visiting. I intentionally tripped over and mispronounced words to make my fake lack of knowledge more believable.

'Huh,' he said, rubbing his chin. 'Plan interest me. You know business deal more than Johnny. Take Johnny with you. Tokyo not good for him. *Do not* come back with nothing.'

His emotionless threat sent chills down my spine. I had to dig deep to find the courage to make my next move.

'I will need the original statue back for reference, as the expert will easily know the difference at the slightest examination, which will lead to suspicion and unwanted questions.'

He grudgingly handed back the original statue. Then, with a flip of his fingers, he motioned for us to leave. I offered my hand, which he touched with calculated disinterest. Turning, I strode out of the bar as confidently as possible, my insides in turmoil and feeling as though my legs were about to buckle. The yakuza's cruel eyes had told me I was just another Johnny to him now.

I was on the brink of running as I moved from the table to the bar exit. In my desperation, I forgot about Johnny. I urgently pushed the door open. The dim alley light was radiant compared to the pit I had just escaped from. Outside, I fled down a side alley to the main road and flopped on a knee-high wall, adrenaline-laced thunder in my ears. Turning my head, I realised Johnny was close behind. He sat next to me, unable to look me in the face.

'I'm sorry. I will explain everything later, but really, this is not my fault. They have my passport. They know my home address. They…' He winced.

'What have you actually done?'

'I'm in debt. Gambling debt.' He cowered unconvincingly.

'I will text you the details of when we leave. But don't tell the woman coming with us any of this. She definitely won't like it and might not go. Try to think of a solution that doesn't involve returning to Tokyo.'

He nodded in agreement, then silently led me to the train station, where we departed without a glance. I could see that his momentary terror had been overtaken by the delusionary hope of a million-to-one shot for survival – widely over-optimistic odds, to say the least. As for me, the plan that had seemed so simple a few hours before now lay shattered with about as much chance of success as weaving air.

Chapter Twenty

I laid on my bed in the Shin Okubo Sekitei Hotel. My backpack was ready for the morning journey to Hokkaidō. I had not texted Johnny the trip details despite his many pleading texts, growing more desperate in fifteen-minute intervals. As tempting as it was to leave Johnny, I realised my "freedom" would be temporary at best. The yakuza would soon be able to track me through the JET placement office records. The yakuza reach was wider and deeper than any other crime syndicate in the world; they had powerful influence over governments.

My fate was sealed now. Even if my lead turned out to be a dead end, my yakuza host had both photos I had given to Johnny and would soon realise that only the University Museum of Tokyo would have experts on Ainu culture. The yakuza gang would be on our trail once they learnt that Chihiro had dropped everything to go north. However I looked at it, Johnny would have go at least as far as Sapporo with us to meet the Ainu expert. Hopefully I would find a way to dump him then, but for now he would be my burden to carry. I would have to keep any knowledge of his gambling debts from Chihiro.

I finally texted Johnny the time and place to meet. Then I texted Chihiro that we were now a trio and rolled over to rest.

With my mind whirling at high speed, it took hours for sleep to come.

As in all bad situations, the morning came too soon and too bright. The bed sheets were rumpled and torn from two mattress corners, the duvet a knotted and uneven mess: witnesses to my light and troubled sleep. I felt hungover, even though I hadn't partied the night before. I showered slowly, but this brought only mild relief. After dressing, I snatched my bag and headed to our rendezvous at Shinjuku Station. I would be just over an hour early, enough time to grab a coffee at Starbucks, where I could pray to the thankless god of caffeine hoping to stimulate my brain to find solution to my seriously mounting problems.

As expected, the station was busy. I texted my accomplices to let them know I was there. Chihiro, the first to arrive, was fresh-faced and lightly dressed, her hair pulled back in a simple ponytail. She had only one medium-size sport bag, which told me she didn't expect this trip to take more than a few days, two of them filled by the monotony of train travel. I decided a sprinkling of light conversation was in order to pass away the time.

'What is Sapporo like? Have you ever been there before?'

She shook her head, the can of soda brought from a nearby vending machine gently sloshing while she sucked on a straw squeezed underneath her front teeth.

'I only meet Professor Haruto when he visits the museum in Tokyo. That used to be every other month for a few weeks or so; he stays with his children when he visits, I believe. He retired barely a year ago from full-time work but still hosts lectures a few times a year around the country.'

'Are you sure he will be able to decode the kanji on the cloth?'

'I hope so. I doubt there's anyone else alive with his collective knowledge. Even the few remaining Ainu would probably struggle because they've spoken and written mostly Japanese for decades. Sure, there are others who have studied the Ainu language and customs, but none with a whole lifetime of scholarly experience.'

This, of course, was not what I wanted to hear. If there was a chance that the professor could not read the kanji, then Johnny – and me, by proxy – would be finished, possibly in the most extreme, literal sense. I had brought my passport in case I needed a quick escape. I knew the Sapporo airport had day flights to all major and some minor Asian cities. I figured Singapore would be best bet as it is halfway home to England. I told Chihiro why this was necessary in a letter I had already written detailing Johnny's betrayal. It was with my passport inside the breast pocket of my coat for easy access if I needed a quick escape.

As if on cue, Johnny waltzed in as if he didn't have a care in the world and this was a situation of his own choosing. Chihiro stood and greeted him with a perfect curtesy bow, which Johnny clumsily mimicked. He was carrying a very small travel bag – either light travel to its most extreme or, more likely, having gambled away his other possessions. They sat a bit awkwardly, staring at me, apparently waiting for me to ignite the conversation. I checked the time to confirm the train was still twenty minutes away, then looked at them.

'Chihiro, what is Sapporo like? I only know it's not as large and grand as Tokyo.'

'I've only passed through there once on my way to a ski trip with my parents. Sapporo is famous more for its micro beer industry and guaranteed winter snows than anything else. I believe that Professor Haruto lives on the outskirts, but getting there will be easy as there is a train station within walking distance. The city is little more than a small hamlet compared to Tokyo.'

'So how long till we meet him?' Johnny asked, injecting himself into the conversation.

I detected desperation in his tone, something akin to a drowning man.

'Tomorrow afternoon. I've booked us into a hotel near the train station to make the commute to his home easier. Speaking of trains, I think we should go to the platform now; better to get there early and avoid the queues.'

So with Chihiro leading the way, setting the pace, and the two males following behind, we reached the platform in time to board the train to Sapporo. I knew there was a good chance I might never see the bright lights of Tokyo again.

Chapter Twenty-One

It is almost fourteen hours from Tokyo to Sapporo, and we expected to arrive around 9:00p.m. Any thrill I had once felt for long-range train travel had evaporated. Now the weight of my present predicament made the journey decidedly uncomfortable. As soon as we sat down, I told them about my previous night's disturbed sleep. I took the inside seat and rested my head against the window, acting like an uncomfortable glazed pillow, leaving them to make small talk that I instantly switched off. I closed my eyes, and the train's gently swaying motion soon rocked me to into a deep sleep.

A soft tap on my shoulder woke me. Chihiro sat next to me, and Johnny was asleep in an opposite seat. Even in my post-slumber state, I detected urgency in her expression. I had barely rubbed the sleep from my eyes before she hurriedly started whispering.

'Your friend Johnny, I think he may be in some sort of trouble.'

'What makes you say that?'

Her statement surprised me. To my knowledge, Johnny had not acted suspiciously after he joined us. I hoped my fake shock had fooled her.

'See his little finger on his left hand? The top half is missing, and he has a plastic tip – poor quality, I might add – to cover the mutilation. That's a trademark of failing the yakuza.'

The game was now well and truly up. I couldn't lie to her anymore in good conscience. I had wrestled with the dilemma since yesterday and could see many advantages for Johnny keeping his secret but no advantage for Chihiro and me. If she knew the whole story, there was a chance she might help me if the endeavour failed. So I quickly told her the abridged version. Her face turned more scornful with each passing sentence. Thankfully, before I could finish, Johnny flopped over, awake, saving me from a suspected savage verbal response.

We arrived in Sapporo dead on 9:00p.m. The summer was decidedly less heavy so far north. Actually, Siberia is only a short hop across the sea at the top tip of Hokkaidō, leaving most of the island entrenched in a mild winter even at the height of summer. Luckily for us, Sapporo is at the southernmost point of the island, so it gets a touch of summer. The train's route ended at Sapporo, so there was no need to rush off. With my back moulded to the contours of the seat after barely moving during the fourteen-hour trip, it was good to have the time to slowly rise and stretch.

Sapporo is a city of less than 2 million people – a hamlet compared to Tokyo's 38 million. Winter sports and breweries are the city's specialities, but it also boasts of large IT and retail stores. Shin-Sapporo Station was nowhere near as grand or crammed as Tokyo's Shinjuku Station. I was relieved by its straightforward concrete simplicity, an exit sign clearly posted on the platform. Chihiro led the way; Johnny and I tried our best to keep up. The hotel was, as Chihiro claimed, only a short walk from the train station. Chihiro had booked us into a backpacker's hostel, Ino's Place, showing her practical side of keeping costs down to a minimum. However, this meant no luxury thrills and few English speakers. The building had been a pre-World War II manor. No doubt it housed a very privileged family before transforming into a chic crash pad for the world's wandering nationalities. Everything from cooking to relaxing had a communal flare to calm the nerves of people from different cultures caged together for the first time. A small library of books in a cascade of languages was a testament to this mix.

Upon entering the hostel, we gave the standard bow. The check-in clerk seemed a bit confused until Chihiro explained our group's multi-ethnic make-up. Her confusion gone, our greeter briskly showed us to our rooms, which happened to be opposite each other. Chihiro had her own room, of course, while Johnny and I shared ours. In the hallway, we decided to wash and change before going out for a quick dinner nearby as the hostel offered basic snacks only. Finally, refreshed and ready, we swooped out of the hostel and into the night like hungry vultures.

Outside, the air had cooled considerably. Night was falling, and the streetlights had flickered to life. The streets were less congested and chaotic than the simplest Tokyo side street. The people looked like those in any other Japanese city. Yet, unlike their southern counterparts, they were proud in their posture and showed none of Tokyo dwellers' wild pretensions or poorly hidden insecurities. The lights of the various hotels and eateries lacked the in-your-face razzmatazz of other cities. Still, they made up for that with their gentle attention to detail.

We approached a building with a striking bright blue façade and large rectangular windows. Compared to its concrete grey neighbours, this place seemed one of a kind. Johnny and I were immediately drawn to its English name: Irish Pub Marman.

Somehow, in this totally foreign land and culture, it felt like we had found a taste of home. It was as though home had been long forgotten and barely remembered, a land 1,000 years in the past and months away in transit. In truth, we had barely spent twelve months away, and home was really a mere hop, skip and jump from the nearest airport.

We entered the establishment and were greeted by bright red walls, the wonderful smell of deep-fried fish, and rows of dripping, foaming pint glasses. We dragged Chihiro along without giving her a chance to protest. She did not try to hide her distaste.

The pub was part of the Centurion Hotel: a five-star masterpiece of marble and velvet decadence. The pub was a grungy little haunt, adding a hint of cultural spice to the hotel's sterile perfection. Chihiro ordered a glass of water, her hunger gone from the fried fish smell. Johnny and I ordered fish and chips. The aroma momentarily carried me back to a seaside holiday during my childhood. Life was simple and easy until I realised my parents' marriage was a sham, but I still remember how I loved fish and chips.

When my dinner came, I had to reacquaint myself with a knife and fork after a year of forced chopsticks. I clumsily sawed the fish and scooped the mushy peas as though suffering from phantom limbs syndrome.

Chihiro excused herself and left for the bathroom, leaving Johnny and me sitting in silence, looking in every direction to avoid looking at each other. When Chihiro came back, we agreed to return to the hostel. As soon as Johnny's back was turned, Chihiro shoved a napkin in my hand, which I swiftly slid into my pocket.

We returned to the hostel and decided to take an early night as our next day would be busy and required an early start.

Johnny and I entered our room, and I headed for the toilet, mainly to read Chihiro's note but also because the two pints of beer I had consumed at the pub were pleading to be expelled. The note was written crudely with what appeared to be an eye liner pencil. The letters were large and clumsily formed, almost as though written by a toddler.

Meet me in my room at 11:00. I will leave the door unlocked.

The time was now about 9:30p.m. I flushed the napkin down the toilet, making sure the clockwise whirlpool properly sucked it down. I returned to the main room to find Johnny laying in his bed looking to be already asleep, his back turned away from me. I slipped under the sheets fully dressed, ready to slip out for my rendezvous with Chihiro, and flicked the lights off. I pulled the covers over my head and played on my phone while waiting for the time to pass. Finally, Johnny's snores broke the silence.

Chapter Twenty-Two

By 10:55p.m., I could no longer stand the boredom or hold my anticipation in check. I was really hot and sure a headache was coming on from light dehydration and cataracts from straining my eyes on the mobile phone screen. I quietly slid out of bed and walked to the door. I gently pulled it open a jot and squeezed through. Light snoring was all that came from Johnny's direction, and I had neither the time nor inclination to check on him. I discreetly slid Chihiro's door open, not bothering to knock as, in the present circumstances, it might ruin the whole espionage vibe. I entered the room to find the lights on yet vacant of life. A TV crackled in the low tones of late-night Japanese shows I could never hope to comprehend.

Because I did not have the right or a reason to venture into the bedroom or bathroom, I sat on the small sofa and watched a game show that needed no translation. The wall clock showed the time as two minutes before 11:00p.m. I decided to wait until at least 11:05p.m. till I attempted to find my absent host as any earlier attempt might appear impolite or rude.

Just as the clock's hands were about to slip to 11:00p.m., Chihiro appeared. She was tightly wrapped in a Western-style dressing gown, killing any idea of our rendezvous turning into an erotic escapade. She sat down opposite me, a cup of green tea in her hand. I watched as she gently blew the mint-scented steam to cool it before taking a sip.

'I have been thinking about our situation,' she said slowly, almost accusingly, with a hint of annoyance. 'I am glad you told me, and I do see why you waited to do so until after I met Johnny so as not to raise his suspicions. But still, the situation is delicate. Which yakuza clan does he work for? Which area of Tokyo did the meeting take place in?'

'They didn't say, and I had no urge to get further acquainted. It was in Koto city on Tokyo's far edge, if that helps.'

Deep frown lines parted her forehead. 'Just as I feared. It's most likely the Inagawa-kai clan. They are the most powerful in Tokyo and one of the largest in the country. They have allies as far north as here. We'll have to be careful as they will probably want to keep track of their investment. I have a suggestion. Do you know where Johnny keeps his mobile phone?'

'Yes, it's charging by the wall in our room as we speak.'

'Good. I want you to go and sabotage it somehow. Maybe pry or damage the casing around the battery so the copper plate or pins no longer make proper contact. He'll find it useless in the morning, and it can easily be blamed on overheating. He won't have time to buy a replacement as we have to head off first thing to see Professor Haruto for an early afternoon appointment. Make sure to bring the statue and canvas with you.'

With a nod towards the doorway, Chihiro indicated the meeting was over, so I got up and readied myself to slip back into my room SAS-style. Polite as always, Chihiro came to the doorway to send me off, yet from the corner on my eye, I noticed a sharp grimace creasing her mouth.

'If you have to contact me tomorrow, text me away from Johnny's prying eyes, only when you're sure he can't see. The napkin was a one-off. From now on, keep your texts from me on silent, and I will do the same with yours. We will meet again tomorrow night in my room, same time, to see how events have progressed.'

With that, she opened the door. I left Chihiro's room and returned to mine.

I slinked over to Johnny's mobile phone, keeping my footsteps in harmony with his snoring, and carefully slipped the mobile phone battery out as instructed. In the dim red light of the bedside's LCD clock, I could barely see the brass plate's soft gleam. As I intended to perform my electronic surgery without any implement to help with the prying, I hoped my right thumbnail would be strong enough to at least bend the plate and snap it out. The low illumination increased my anxiety. With every passing second, I grew more nervous that Johnny would wake up and discover my ploy. Luckily, the phone was cheap, and after a couple of attempts, the brass tips bent, and a solid flick snapped the edge off. I replaced the battery pack and clicked it on. Yes! The phone was now totally unresponsive. I breathed a sigh of relief. After hastily shuffling my clothes off under the sheets of my bed, I promptly fell into a deep slumber.

Chapter Twenty-Three

The morning came too soon. My head was heavy from sleep deprivation, the web of deceit I had woven, and the fear that recent events could easily unpluck my future with the slightest misstep. Through my half-open right eye, I saw Johnny studying his phone. He was trying to shake it back to life, checking if the power cord was inserted and fiddling with the plug socket, hoping his barrage of insults would resuscitate the phone from the brink. I rose and quickly showered and dressed before hurrying Johnny out with me. In defeat, he left his phone behind. We grabbed a quick breakfast of cold toast and lukewarm coffee. I went for a smoke, hoping the cool fresh air would sharpen my senses.

It was barely 8:15a.m. when Chihiro joined us outside. I had the statue and canvas in my backpack as well as my passport and enough money to book a flight from Sapporo if I needed to escape quickly. We headed to the train station to catch a quick five-mile ride to the outer suburbs of Kita-ku and Professor Haruto. He was the only one who could unravel the truth behind our endeavour. If he failed, we'd be sunk.

The train jerked out of Shin-Sapporo Station running on old rolling stock rather than the magnetic grace of the rail that had brought us here from Tokyo. We rattled out of Sapporo and into its sprawling suburbs filled with concrete houses intercut with billboards that could have been in any Tokyo alley or cul-de-sac. I found it slightly depressing that such a creative culture, nurtured from 300 years of isolation from the other main islands, had such little regard for Japanese architectural design. The buildings may be practical for earthquake protection, but they hurt my eyes. No attempt had been made to doll them up in the slightest with a lick of paint or hint of originality. They were just rows and rows of the same ugly, plain, Western-style dwellings. As we gained distance from Sapporo's centre, the number of houses decreased. Those we could see from the train became larger and older until finally devolving into the traditional wooden Japanese-style structures. It was almost like travelling back in time. The houses sat neatly along each side of the tracks. Obviously, some had been demolished to make room for the tracks laid over one hundred years ago, all in the name of progress. After travelling about twenty-five minutes, the train pulled into our stop and we got off the train.

It was clear by Ainosato-kōen Station's elegantly simple design and the upper-class attire of the casual passers-by that this was the high-end of town. The wide roads and large detached houses were further testament to that. Chihiro had written instructions to guide her, but despite being Japanese, she struggled with the chaotic postcode system. In old-style Japan, street postcodes were designated by original construction date, not the land layout order. This was challenging to even the most veteran of postmen, and a detailed map is often essential to find one's way. After wandering aimlessly and asking a few bemused locals for directions, we finally found the professor's neighbour on his afternoon stroll. He set us straight, and within minutes we arrived at our destination.

The wooden gates were painted white and perfectly preserved, which was quite an accomplishment given Sapporo's harsh annual climate. I suspected the upkeep was expensive. As we passed through the gates with a gentle click, the harsh crunch of gravel echoed underfoot as we walked the path through a pristine garden holding flourishes of deep purples and explosions of glorious oranges. Even the most common of Japanese summer plants radiated like a barrage of organic fireworks. The house had survived numerous earthquakes and avoided the scars of Japan's internal and external wars over the past 200 years. Its perfect white wooden-panel walls and red-tiled roof were found only in homes whose owners spend a lifetime taking care of them. We reached the door and Chihiro gave it a short, sharp knock. From beyond, an aged voice beckoned us to enter.

Professor Haruto welcomed us with the traditional strong bow, which we clumsily returned. He was a short man with deep grey hair and large eyebrows protruding like a canopy over his eyes, shading them from the glare of the late morning sun. His face showed age, but his body was as slim and agile as a man two decades younger. We took our shoes off, as is customary. He showed us into a traditional Japanese reception room with spotless, polished wooden floors and walls framed with Shōji paper. He invited us to sit on a cushioned futon at the room's centre. Bookshelves lined the walls, a lifetime of reading bound in leather. In places, the bookshelves parted to provide space for display cases of broken bowls and half-eroded stone tools, all on pedestals with display lights acting like miniature halos to dispel shadows and show off the pieces. He serenely served us tea, yet I could see that behind his mannerisms, burning eyes focused on my bag. Clearly, eighty-plus years of ridged politeness training was under strain from his urge to see my discovery.

While I unwrapped my find and Chihiro stood in awe within the professor's academic spell, Johnny surveyed the room with the look of a burglar casing the joint. The professor's priceless antiques dominated his attention. Carefully, I lifted the statue out of my backpack and handed it to the professor. Then I unfolded the cloth and spread it out as best I could on the table next to us. He studied the statue with his right eye and the canvas with his left, like a child struggling to choose between presents on Christmas morning. With his free hand, he pulled a notebook off a shelf in the bookcase beside him. After intently turning is pages, he finally placed the statue back on the table. I could see him trying to match up his own research with my relic. He flicked the notebook pages back and forth, matching the canvas markings with the equivalent Japanese kanji in his notebook, as though playing an academic game of snap.

'The statue is an orca whale called *Repun Kamuy*, *Kamuy* being the Ainu word for god. I believe it and many other artifacts were confiscated during the Meiji Restoration from the Ainu then ironically stolen in the 1870s on tour with the fabled Tokugawa Treasure. The canvas is a sort of code. The author only knew the basics of Japanese kanji. At best, the average person today would only have a fifty-fifty chance of deciphering the message. All evidence considered, there's little doubt the poor person was from the coast of Hokkaidō.'

'Can you make it out?' I gasped.

Everyone was suffering from the atmosphere of anticipation for vastly different reasons.

'I can, but it will take some time. I am going to take some high-resolution digital pictures of each letter backed by a light box, which should cut through any dirt and distortion. As you know, I have an appointment this afternoon, but I will use every free moment I have today to decipher it and will send you what I find tonight.'

He took photos of the statue and canvas, gave the artefacts back to me, then slipped out his camera's memory card and placed it into his pocket. Eager to leave for his appointment, he picked up his notebook and escorted us out of the house. He jumped into his car, and before careening off, he thanked us sincerely for the chance to investigate our find.

As the professor drove off, we realised we were now at loose ends until he shared his conclusions. The tension between us was so dense that even passers-by stared before getting out of our way. But maybe this was just my budding paranoia.

We walked back to Shin-Sapporo Station. As we entered, Johnny announced he was going to try and find somewhere to fix his phone, which he had brought with him after all. He departed quickly, leaving Chihiro and me to wander the station and return to Sapporo without him.

'He doesn't need to get his phone fixed. He can soon buy a new one with the same service provider. All it has done is bought us some time. We have to assume he's going to report everything back to the yakuza,' Chihiro pointed out.

'We could say that the professor finds nothing conclusive, then head back to Tokyo and vanish into the night,' I quickly suggested.

'That sounds like a plan. I'll return later after you and Johnny are long gone and the situation's safer,' Chihiro replied with a wide smile.

Chihiro said that now all there was to do was to play the waiting game. She looked at the train timetables for Tokyo while I monitored flight schedules to anywhere but Japan. For the remainder of the afternoon, we felt a brief air of normality compared to the past few days. We were both at a loss and didn't know what to do. Only the professor had the ability to set events back on track. We felt as though our lives were spinning out of control like a car clutch searching for the biting point.

Back in Sapporo, Chihiro and I wandered the streets in silence, bound by an artificial bond of deceit, betrayal and fear. I was anxious for the whole episode to be over. I kept checking my jacket pocket to confirm my passport and bank card were there and available at a moment's notice if needed. Half-interestedly, we took in a few of the local tourist sites. First, we visited the Toyohira River Ryokuchi Park. It was a strip of green crawling along the banks of the Toyohira River which wandered through the city. The river water reflected the city's cement grey gloom and the park's dense patches of trees sheltering us from the noon heat. Next, we headed to the Shiroishi Shrine, more a religious complex then a humble shrine. A large, peaked-roof wooden temple commanded the complex's centre. Dozens of Torii gates and bridges crossed perfectly sculptured streams. A man-sized stone dragon looked down at us, its eyes eternality open.

These were interesting and beautiful sites, yet their wonders could barely distract us from our agonised anticipation of the professor's results. We decided to return to our hostel and wait for the professor's message, our collective fate riding on his expertise.

Chapter Twenty-Four

As we rounded the corner into the street of our hostel, we heard someone loudly shouting Chihiro's name in a heavy Japanese accent in symphony with someone shouting mine with an unmistakable Australian twang. Chihiro and I turned, almost in unison, to find Professor Haruto and Johnny sharing tea under a parasol in the outside court of a "traditional" Japanese tearoom. This place catered almost solely to tourists. Mock teenage geishas in cheap ill-fitting kimonos, their glazed eyes showing they would rather be anywhere else but there, served the tourist tea-drinkers.

We went over and sat opposite the two. When I saw the professor's excited expression filled with new youthful energy, I strongly suspected the exit plan Chihiro and I had devised a mere hour ago was about to change. Like a galloping wild horse, the professor started speaking, his words falling one after the other, the vowels thundering, their syllables barely in sync.

'The script on the canvas is an Ainu kanji in its most rawest of forms. It doubles both as a haiku and a riddle. It seems the message may have been for some other member of the tribe. Or maybe the writer didn't fully grasp even the basics of language structure, literally stuck in the middle, fighting between two different alphabets. This would explain the mangled mix of Japanese and Ainu kanji telling them how to find where the other statues are hidden or where the trail to these treasures begins. Two hundred years ago, this information would have been worthless without detailed local knowledge and a small army, but now, with Hokkaidō fully mapped in great detail, it should be easy to find or, at the very least, modestly achievable. Chihiro, this discovery would make your career, and you and Mike would be foreign heroes. If only I were thirty years younger, I would be ready for the task, but this is a mission for youth, not me.'

'But surely they would have been found years ago?' I enquired.

'Do not mistake grainy satellite images to be the same as fully mapped on the ground. There are still many areas in the dense forest and deep canyons of the north where few, if anyone, have stepped foot for decades, maybe centuries, for the simple lack of a good reason to go on such a far-flung folly. I can show you the starting point: the coastal town of Utorokogen on the Shiretoko Peninsula, the furthest northern tip of Hokkaidō. Fittingly, the Ainu called it the End of the Earth. Catch a train from Sapporo Station to the town of Shari, and from Shiretoko-Shari Station take a brief bus trip to Utorokogen, and you can be at the starting point easily within a day. As it's the height of summer, you only need the most basic of camping supplies. A modern map and compass will make getting lost close to impossible. Never could so much be within grasp with such little effort!'

'And what does the canvas's poem say?' asked Johnny.

The professor cleared his throat, and with the hushed tone of an aged mystic, he began his mantra:

'Start from the nest of rocks near the tip of the peak which touches the heavens, between the cradle of the sun and the alter of the moon, and, looking over the tip of the earth, between the scars of age, follow the tears of the mountain, look through the ageless eye which is eaten by time, find the island that appears purely by its own whim. All life is caught between the devil and the dusk. The largest peak on the Shiretoko Peninsula is Mount Rausu, which also doubles as an Ainu pilgrimage site. This could possibly be "the nest of rocks on the peak". I suggest you start there.'

With that, the professor departed. We sat in stunned silence, our course now dictated by events set in motion centuries before we were born. The professor had left a map circling the starting position. The map was quite general, its details largely absent. Apart from showing rivers and unnatural, angular blocks of woods, there were few fine details such as contour ridges or power lines. The professor was right: the map was unhelpfully obscure.

To prepare for our journey into the unknown, we made up a shopping list. By the time we finished, the afternoon had turned to early evening. We decided to split up to do our shopping in the early morning to prepare for our afternoon departure. Johnny and I would buy the camping equipment while Chihiro would arrange train tickets. Satisfied with our accomplishment, we resolved to have dinner to celebrate at our previous destination – the Irish Pub Marman. Johnny bought us a sake round to celebrate, and after far too many, we merrily staggered back to our hostel. It appeared as though Johnny had forgotten his desperation.

Chapter Twenty-Five

I awoke in semi-darkness with a right eye knitted two-thirds closed and a blinding headache. The stench of vomit and sweat grated my nostrils, causing me to retch again on a now totally empty stomach. The heave brought my formerly dormant limbs back to life in violent spasms, shaking stiff legs and sharpening the pounding in my head.

I sat up on my bed, still fully dressed, and stared into the opposite mirror. I saw the face of what looked like a recently thrashed brawler squinting back at me. My knuckles were layered in a thin scab. It was impossible to say if the war scene was due to a violent impact with another face or harsh scrapes from a fall. I pressed and probed my right eye, almost swollen shut and bruised black. The area around it showed a crisscross of tiny cuts. I was about to stand when the bathroom door opened and a less bruised but equally pale and sickly Johnny appeared, shaking and spasming like a fish marooned in the centre of a desert.

'You awake?' he asked in a shocked tone as if I had suddenly risen from the grave.

I found that slightly distressing. Before I could ask what had happened, he read the confusion on my face and began to enlighten me.

'After the professor left us at the tearoom, we decided to go back to the Irish Pub Marman to toast our good fortune. We had a few drinks and something to eat, and before we knew it, you had disappeared. I found you vomiting into the toilets, and after a few minutes of trying to help you, I, too, began projectile vomiting. In the end, we were tossed out into the street by security. That's the last thing I remember before waking up ten minutes ago to throw up the last remnants of my stomach lining.'

I listened to his summary of the previous night's events but could only recall leaving the Japanese tearoom, not the Irish pub. Then I remembered that Chihiro had been there, too. It was at that point that she practically fell through our door, the same drained, confused look on her face.

Johnny reiterated his tale to Chihiro. She confirmed that she had the same symptoms and vomiting. Despite still feeling terrible, we all agreed to shower and change before going to get the blandest breakfast we could find and finish preparations for our expedition.

We were in the hostel's kitchen eating the vending machine's gourmet delights of preheated canned coffee and Styrofoam cup noodles, hoping to ease our ravaged stomachs. As I emptied my second can of coffee, probably out of muscle memory, I unconsciously reached inside my jacket pocket, only to find my passport missing. The shock almost caused me to regurgitate my recent meal. Perhaps my two companions would have noticed my extreme distress if they had not already been distracted by the continued physical distress of their own bodies.

***

Chihiro insisted we stick to the schedule as if sickness was no excuse for delay. We were to ignore our vomiting troubles and split up as planned. Chihiro left to buy the train tickets, her mental skills seemingly more focused than Johnny and I put together. My head was a light whirl, my limbs painfully heavy, my higher cognitive function numbed to the lowest level of autopilot. I drifted into a waking nightmare, only able to focus on the task at hand. Johnny seemed slightly less affected as he led me like a lamb up and down the alleys and between the streams of people. Part of me knew I should be more concerned about my missing passport. Still, that voice struggled to be heard over the suffocating weight of my foggy mind, all common sense drowned out by my desire to begin our journey. I had no will left to contemplate the future after the next few days. Every step seemed a burden; every store visit was a momentous task. We finally found a place that spoke passable English and would deliver our purchases directly to our hotel. After asking us basic questions, the sales rep quickly picked out items we needed. This was a godsend, as though we had been drowning and a pallet of driftwood had saved us.

Johnny and I then retired to our hotel for a few hours of deep rest. The train left at 7:00p.m., giving our trio two hours to our destination, Utorokogen, where we would stay the night before beginning our adventure the next day. To no avail, Chihiro had been trying to ring the professor to see if he, too, had been taken ill. She tried one final time just before the train departed to the outer wilds of Hokkaidō, where mobile phone coverage would be weak to none. He didn't answer.

Part Three

Chapter Twenty-Six

According to the professor, the area around Utorohigashi village had been inhabited by the Ainu people for over a millennium due to its easy fishing and rich, game-filled forest. It was likely this was the origin of the cave corpse I had found off the south coast of Hagi and whose canvas poem had unintentionally pointed us here. He had set sail for a new life from this very port before fate dealt him a final blow.

The train took us from Sapporo to Shari town, crawling at a leisure pace along the Hokkaidō coastal spine. Shari town was our last stop before setting out for Utorohigashi village. The trip would be mercifully brief compared to my other recent train journeys, yet my mind was sour knowing that I now had no real chance of escape. With my passport gone, only finding the other statues would help me now.

The sea air's salty stench was so vivid the moment we exited the train at Utorohigashi, it almost knocked me sick. My nostrils and sinuses had become accustomed to the toxic dry vapours of the city. I had forgotten the strong, dank smells of the world's miraculous seas.

We were to spend the night here, a coastal village dominated by a vast harbour creeping along the coast. The only other highlights were a half-dozen local sightseeing spots with little else apart from the mandatory shops and Shinto shrines. Before the next day's early morning start, I needed a full night's sleep to recuperate. I doubted I could cope with any more travelling without losing my temper or my stomach.

Chihiro had booked us into the local Ainu Inn of Shūchou no Ie. On the Shiretoko Peninsula, an Ainu chief owned this inn. Decked out in traditional Ainu style, it was as ancient and preserved as the Roman Colosseum. Its wooden-panel wall, frozen for centuries, was perfectly preserved by handed-down methods. The stone floors were worn smooth by millions of footsteps from thousands of patrons over generations. Even the oil heating system could have been installed in Victorian times. The inn boasted a museum with a variety of textiles woven with rainbows of neon to tell the stories of Ainu folklore deities, such as Akkorokamui, the benevolent Kraken who had the powers to heal and bestow knowledge. The textiles also told the story of the Korpokkur, a race of small people who lived on the land before the Ainu. They hated to be seen and were on good terms with the Ainu. They would send the Ainu people deer, fish, and other game in exchange for Ainu goods. One day, a young Ainu man decided he wanted to see a Korpokkur for himself, so he waited in ambush by the window where they usually left their gifts. When a Korpokkur came to place something there, the young man grabbed it by the hand and dragged it inside. It turned out to be a beautiful Korpokkur woman who was so enraged at the young man's rudeness that her people had not since been seen. The textiles also celebrated dozens of other *kamuy* – Ainu divine beings from Shiramba: the humble *kamuy* of wood, grains, and other vegetation, and the menacing *Pauchi Kamuy* born from the Willow-Soul River in Pikun Kando (High Heaven). The *Pauchi Kamuy* descended to earth to plague humanity with insanity, stomach ailments, food poisoning, seizures, frenzied dancing – and life's other "cheerful" calamities.

Musical instruments, made from a no-doubt painstaking process long lost to time, including stretched-skin drums and sinew tendon stringed guitars to hollowed-out bone flutes. Black-and-white photos of a long-dead orchestra filled the walls, the musicians forever remembered in that timeless moment. Lastly, and of most interest to us, was a row of life-sized Ainu pattern sculptures of Hokkaidō's wildlife, from a quietly sleeping mouse to a black bear, his jaws open in brutal anticipation.

Chihiro had told us that the inn had hot, spring-fed baths infused with eons of aged minerals. She said the superstitious believed these minerals could draw out any illness and soothe all ailments – absorption and rehydration being the spring's chief remedies. Only half-listening at the time, I thought a bath in the hot spring might settle me before bed. I decided to take one at some point in the evening.

We ate our evening meal in the inn's small restaurant, a selection of home-made traditional Ainu meals. We tasted an assortment of local fish and vegetables mixed with rice. The food's general blandness was a blessing as it layered our stomachs, still recovering from the stretching and swelling of our previous mutual vomiting marathon. After we finished our meal, Johnny declared he was going for a walk around town to see the sights for a few hours before bed. I suspected his real intent was to find the nearest bar and try to bury his troubles in an avalanche of cheap sake.

Chihiro had booked the only two rooms on the top floor with barely enough space for two single futons. The one bathroom was a definite plus. It came with a private, traditional, open-air bath with hot water piped up from the spring below. The hot, spring-fed bath, just barely able to accommodate four people comfortably, was more than adequate for myself. I gently slipped in, hoping the milky mineral water would sooth my remaining aches.

I leant back and stretched my legs to their full length. The water came halfway up my chin. A calm tiredness replaced the stinging stress of the long day. As I soaked, my mind replayed the alarming events that had left me stranded in rural Japan. For the foreseeable future, with no passport and no money, I had no way to escape.

I was on the verge of light sleep in the warm water when I became aware that I was no longer alone. I opened one eye a crack to see the briefly descending and completely naked Chihiro merging into the bath opposite me. I was just in time to have the fortune of seeing her erect nipples sink into the milky minerals. I was annoyed that my tiredness had robbed me of the pleasure of seeing her fully naked. I was now totally awake, all my facilities at hardened attention.

'I hope you don't mind me joining you, there are matters we must urgently discuss.'

Those were possibly the two most understated phrases I had heard that day.

'It's about the food poisoning. I've been thinking it over. Do you think Johnny drugged us?' she asked in a hushed tone.

'That seems a bit extreme,' I stammered.

'Think about it – he got the drinks for us and could have easily slipped something in. Only he can remember going to the bar, and we only have his word for the rest of his story. The yakuza could have given him some sort of drug before we left Tokyo.'

'But to what end? What advantage was there for him…'

I felt her toes sliding up, leg to thigh, before finally resting on my crotch.

'To take your passport, strand you here. Your lack of other options would bind you to him, your only hope to focus on finding the statues. He must have seen you put it in your jacket or checked when you weren't looking.'

Chihiro's foot was now slowly caressing my manhood up and down, instantly engulfing my mind into a lustful smog. My own foot then began gently rubbing her womanhood. Chihiro's breasts moved out the water as she massaged them in rhythm with each increasingly stronger rub of my foot. This lasted a few minutes but seemed like mere moments, the ecstasy building in both of us. Suddenly she threw her arms open and spread her legs wide, her knees ramming the side of the tub. I moved into her arms and entered her, pounding, the water frothing with each thrust, causing larger and more violent waves that soon spilled over the side. It was our own private, passionate tsunami. Like an earthquake, with two loud moans – our "all-clear" sirens – it finished as abruptly as it had started. We remained in each other's arms for a moment longer, letting me shrink inside her before we both pushed away.

'I have wanted that since I first saw you,' she whispered before abruptly changing the subject as though a different person. 'Tomorrow, we go into the mountains, and if Johnny returns treasure-laden or empty-handed, it will make little difference. He will still be our curse. The solution is that we lose him up there, one way or another, hopefully after finding the statues, and slip away into the night. I bought an extra map I will keep on myself at all-times. Be ready to move when the moment's right.'

As she stood up and turned to go, I watched the milky mineral water roll down her naked body as though caressing it. Almost as an afterthought, she wrapped a towel around herself and left as quickly as she had arrived, leaving me alone with roaring emotions.

I returned to my room to lie on my bed and review in my mind the just-transpired scenario. I concluded that – like all unplanned events in life – while the passion had been too brief to be fully appreciated, her quick departure without even the slightest backward glance revealed a mechanical desire on her part, perhaps born more out of physical necessity than for emotional connection. That thought was as thrilling as it was oddly spine-chilling.

I was in the middle of these warm-filled thoughts when Johnny stumbled into our room slightly tipsy but a league away from total intoxication. He flopped down in his bed. I knew a barrage of drunken banter was on its way.

'I've been thinking, and I reckon Chihiro may have drugged us both last night.'

Of all the things I thought he would say, I expected that statement the least.

'What makes you say that?'

'Chihiro claims she was sick last night, yet there was little evidence of it this morning, and I've watched her closely all day. There has been no lack of appetite and no real hints of fatigue on her part.'

He leant close and our heads almost bumped accidentally.

'I know you told her of my situation: you have no skill for deceit or lying. Remember, while that sort of honesty may be a virtue, it can easily be used against you. In those mountains, we need to be on our guard. Chihiro is native to these parts with all the aces up her sleeve, and we could soon be as disposable as joker cards if and when we find the artefacts. A woman with that level of drive and ambition will not brake for anyone or suffer the slightest deviation.'

With that parting piece of wisdom, Johnny turned and went to sleep. Soon, the familiar rambling of his snoring was the only soundtrack to my racing mind.

It dawned on me that I knew little of real substance about either of my companions. Both had valid reasons and needs to find the statues. Either one of them could have taken my passport to trap me in their company. One could be the poisoner with the other lying to cover their tracks. Or, more realistically, rather than betrayal by either of them, I might have lost my passport while staggering around drunk and poisoned from the food we had eaten.

The tension of my partners' suspicions and revelations in any other circumstance would, no doubt, have kept my mind agile all night, revisiting these events. Tonight, though, my body had been pleasantly drained from frenzied sex. Mercifully, sleep swallowed me whole.

Chapter Twenty-Seven

I awoke the next day deeply rested and fully recuperated. I pushed the unpleasant thoughts of betrayal and poison out of mind. My better judgement tried in vain to impose some common sense on everything. My post-coital glow of happy satisfaction wanted to drown out those thoughts. There was no urgency in our preparations as we split the camping equipment into three roughly equal loads. We had bought the lightest and cheapest equipment we could find. Lucky for us, on the food front, the Japanese have mastered the art of lightweight dehydrated meals, so there was no need for heavy tin cans or other bulky produce apart from our water bottles. The three of us looked as out of place as a family of polar bears leaning on a palm tree. We had a strong, traditional Ainu breakfast of fresh fish and vegetables dipped in rich sauce to brace us for the days ahead. Our last taste of real vegetables and fresh fish would soon be replaced by plain rice and shrivelled, dehydrated bread husks mushed together into a weak-flavoured goo. We left just after 10:00a.m. and trekked out to the edge of Utorohigashi. Within fifteen minutes, we had left the tarmac roads, concrete homes and every other hint of civilization behind us.

Our first destination was the summit of Mount Tenchozan. It was seven kilometres away and just over 1,000 metres high. We climbed up a deep valley cut out of the earth by a now-anaemic river. The area had been a volcanic heartland just under 2,000 years ago. The tepid hot springs were the last testament of the area's magma-fury past. A few light veins of igneous rock were now clutched and shattered from the grip of centuries-old tree roots. The forest at each side of the valley was so dense that its canopy trapped most of the sun's light, imprisoning an infinite number of mysteries waiting to be discovered and set free. Noting this, I began to understand how archaeological finds like the statues could be hidden all this time. Under such an expanse of uncorrupted nature, anything was possible.

We crossed a stream through a shallow ford and headed out of the forest's gloom, finally remerging into the hard afternoon light. Tenchozan Peak, our first point of call, was directly in front of us. Hopefully its panoramic view would let us match the first line of the poem with its namesake in the natural world. The mountain top was small and harshly steep. The muscles in the back of my legs began pulling painfully with every stride. Just when I thought they were on the verge of snapping, we finally reached the peak. The top layer of shale was so dense it created a barrier against vegetation growth, thus keeping the tree line a good twenty feet below the peak. Still, after centuries, a few tree roots had amazingly managed to scratch through the area in weak protest.

'Start from the nest of rocks near the tip of the peak which touches the heavens...'

From the top of Tenchozan Peak, we could see Mount Rausu, by far the highest peak on the Shiretoko Peninsula. Just under 4.5km north, we could see a grey stone peak sprinkled in green foliage – its only hint of colour on the mountain towering proudly above the rest. We headed towards Mount Rausu along a ridge that ran like a spine, each bump like a vertebra. We picked our way along the flimsy path, following its slope up to Rausu's throne, our shadows shrinking by the hour as the day heated up. After reaching the top of Mount Rausu, our first real test was about to begin.

'…Between the cradle of the sun and the alter of the moon, and, looking over the tip of the earth.'

That was our first clue. Unfortunately for us, it was shrouded in vagueness, almost proudly. Somewhere in the vast expanse of mountains, valleys, streams and rocks that lay before us was, conceivably, the beginning of the trail to the statues, bringing us collective glory – or time-wasted folly.

It was around midday, and we stopped for some lunch. We had enough supplies to last two days at most. We could see a few coastline farms scattered around to contact if an emergency occurred and the situation vastly deteriorated. Personally, I was still fifty per cent sure this was nothing but a wild goose chase, and the golden goose had been dead for decades before we were born.

'Is there some special meaning to the sun cradle and moon altar in Japanese?' Johnny asked Chihiro.

We were feasting on tuna sandwiches, our one gourmet luxury before the dirge of noodle pots washed down by water from our aluminium canteens.

'They are both mentioned numerous times in old folklore and poems. Yet I can't recall them phrased in such abstract terms. Remember, the person who wrote this was Ainu, which is a whole different culture. Their religion and laws are based on beliefs separate from the Japanese. You both know as much as me on the subject. All our insights are equal.'

The conversation stopped there, and we finished lunch soon after. We decided to check the mountainside for clues and split up. I headed right, and Johnny and Chihiro went left. I scanned around the base rocks looking for some sort of deliberate marking or naturally occurring anomaly. The course rock surface left no shine that generations of polishing footsteps would have left. That got me thinking that perhaps the professor had identified the wrong hill. It may be a famous local landmark, but Mount Rausu was admired more from afar than used close-up as a place of devote pilgrimage.

I walked away from them, found a warm rock and decided to lay down on it for a quick skive. Perhaps the massaging heat would ease my thighs' muscle cramps and inspire a revelation about the riddle, untangling itself in my mind's eye. I held out my outstretched hand, fingers spread apart, and watched the sun slowly creep between their gaps from full throttle to total eclipse. I was the master of my own private solar system! With my free middle finger, I tracked the sun's path and discovered that it would settle almost perfectly on the peak of one of the distant mountains to the west. I lazily started to count the mountains, going from left to right, to find an even twelve with twenty-three valleys between. The first haiku line was still cycling in the back of my mind when I heard the crunch of steps. I turned to see Chihiro and Johnny approaching. Their faces revealed they were no nearer to a solution than me.

'There are twelve peaks from this spot; that's the only distinguishing fact I can see from this point,' I wearily stated.

'Both the sun and moon rise from the east and set in the west,' Johnny obviously pointed out.

'And there are twenty-four hours in the day, which can roughly be split into two twelve-hour periods for argument's sake,' Chihiro added.

'Did the Ainu even know the days were twelve hours long?' Johnny asked.

I said, 'Let's assume they did. The tip of the earth must be the point of the Shiretoko Peninsula, pointing to the sea you can make out in the distance. The cradle would be the farthest western peak running along the coast, and the altar would be the middle peak of the twelve, meaning the valley we need is the first on this peak's west or left side. This would be our path.'

Johnny and Chihiro followed my pointed finger to the route we would take down into the densely wooded valley, which looked no more exotic than its neighbouring siblings. We looked over the map to see where the valley led, yet everything eventually ended at the coast. This meant that if we made a mistake, we could backtrack if needed, and all might not be lost. None of us was even vaguely optimistic about this path, but with no other option, we pressed on.

The slope to the valley below was steep, and we proceeded on tired, unsteady legs. The slope was naked apart from wispy, wind-blasted grass and clumps of cowering shrubs, the raw elements having long strip-mined the ground of any life. The valley vegetation greeting our weary approach was in stark contrast to Mount Rausu's rapier peak. Towering ridges along the valley's sides sheltered flora from nature's extremes. A dense canopy of trees trapped the warm sunny air, casting a macabre early afternoon twilight gloom over everything.

We entered the canopy just after noon. Unseen birds hid in the tall branches, tweeting and announcing our arrival, blotting out the hushed silence of the hill. The forest floor was thick with fallen leaves, twigs and branches, making a crunchy carpet that gnashed with every footstep. Dim light meant there were few plants other than the occasional smear of moss on some large boulders protruding from the swamp of tree debris. According to the map, a nearby small river led from the valley to the sea. We looked around and found a gently trickling stream illuminated by a strip of sunlight in the distance. The soil on its banks was too thin for trees to grow, but a riot of multicoloured wildflowers had created a floral oasis instead.

'If we assume that the valley is the scar of the earth and the river is its trail of tears, then we should follow the river towards the sea to see what we can find.'

'A waterfall, perhaps?' I speculated.

'That would be my guess, but there are dozens of waterfalls in that area. There must be something special or unique about this one if it leads to the "ageless eye", whatever that could be.'

'How long do you think it will take till we reach the coast?'

'If we keep a steady pace, I think we can reach the coast by nightfall. We can't rush too much because there's a chance of a clue along the river.'

The time passed quickly, and our pace was slow. When we finally reached the stream, the heat had leached the life out of us. Our only reprieve was the stream's cool water. We filled our canteens and dunked our heads under the rippling water, momentarily submerging our troubles and drowning our discomforts. We stayed close to the halo of light bathing the stream. A low darkness flanked its sides, punctured only by rare sunlight rays shining through odd holes that natural forces had punched through the forest canopy above.

Chapter Twenty-Eight

We were halfway through the seven-kilometre trek, following the stream to the sea, when we decided to stop for a break by a small side pool. It was as good a place as any for a break. As soon as we stopped, our footstep echoes ceased and silence descended. We had seen little wildlife here, which left an eerie feeling that something was different, just out of the reach of our senses.

I sat with Chihiro while Johnny walked off, either out of boredom or to relieve himself. I didn't ask.

'How much longer do you think it will be?' I asked, breaking the silence.

'If we are lucky and keep a good pace, we should reach the shore around early evening. The real question is what to do when we get there. The Ainu words may be poetic, but its vagueness is hardly helpful. Where has Johnny gone?'

As if on cue (timed almost to the point of rehearsal), Johnny remerged from the forest gloom with a smile so wide it threatened to tear the corners of his cheeks. He carried something round, brown and fluffy. He unwrapped it on a nearby rock as though it was a stage. Johnny's whole life had always been a series of insincere performances, fitting his persona for each one's target audience.

The thing raised its head and looked around in a daze. It showed no excitement or fear at the human audience, just pure bewilderment. It licked it nose and scratched its left ear, sitting unsteadily upright on the rock just a soft breeze away from toppling.

'I'd like you both to welcome our new mascot and member of our small intrepid group of explorers slash adventurers.'

The bear cub stared back, neither honoured nor impressed with us. I stood there gobsmacked at Johnny's total lack of sense or reason, knowing only a city boy with no common sense about nature could be that stupid. Clearly, he hadn't bothered to read the leaflet at the Ainu Inn in Utorokogen listing dangerous animals to avoid. Chihiro's horrified look was magnificent to behold. She threw her backpack over her shoulder with such desperate force she almost toppled over from the momentum.

'We have to leave right now! Leave the bear cub there and wash yourself off in the pool. Hopefully, you're not too late to mask your scent!'

Before Johnny could reply, a thunderous roar behind him cut our conversation down in its prime. A stampeding echo of heavy steps filled the air, growing louder and more desperate by the moment. A brown mass grew larger fast as it ran towards us, dodging between the trees with the dexterity of a ballerina and ferocity of a gale-force storm. We were all stunned stupid for a moment before our brains snapped back into gear and our primal instinct for self-preservation kicked in. The massive mother bear, her jaws clashing, sent us careening in different directions with no thought but saving our own hides.

I ran deeper into the forest. The deafening drumming in my ears and galloping of my heart blocked out to all other noise. I was too frightened to turn around, my fear pressing me on at full speed ahead. Finally, my legs buckled, having burned too long and bright on adrenaline-laced acceleration. I turned to see if one of nature's greatest predators was following, making it my fate to be killed and dragged into the bowels of Hokkaidō, never to be seen again.

The forest was empty. The bear was nowhere to be seen, but neither were Johnny or Chihiro. As my pulse subsided, I heard the river tinkling gently in the distance. Having finally caught my breath, it occurred to me that I should search for the other two. At that moment, a piercing, sky-ripping scream slammed me to attention and pointed me in the direction to search.

I crouched and stalked closer to the noise, trying to keep low and downwind (the only stalking clichés from Hollywood that I knew). Looking up, I found Chihiro, who had managed to climb a tree. For some reason, the bear made no effort to climb the tree. Instead, she was trying to shake her prey out of the tree with battering-ram slaps, her claws stripping and slashing the bark as she waited for her human fruit to fall.

I needed a plan, and fast. I could see that Chihiro's grip was weakening with every bear swipe. If she let go, she would fall like bait into the bear's jaws. I hid behind a large boulder and, picking up a few of its cast-off siblings, threw them behind the bear. They hit a tree about twenty feet away with a collision that echoed as bluntly as an artillery barrage.

The bear spun around, tearing her attention from Chihiro. Chihiro, half sobbing and praying the reprieve would last, bolstered her hold for the next assault while the bear investigated the source of noise. She sniffed the air, her eyes scanning for new threats. Disappointed, she returned to the tree for a final assault with a loud snort – a testament to her bravado.

As my plan had failed miserably, I suspected the same trick would have diminished results. I needed a plan B, and quick, with a guaranteed win. I racked my brain for something that would inflict blind fear on the bear.

Chihiro's screams grew louder by the moment. I saw the bear preparing to make her final attack, her afternoon meal now all but guaranteed. An idea broke through my paralysis. With no time to lose, I grabbed my bag, scattered its contents on the ground and grasped a T-shirt. I snatched a nearby stick, desperately wrapping and knotting the t-shirt around it. Then, pushed on by Chihiro's petrified screams, I seized the paraffin from our camp cooking stoves and soaked the t-shirt as best I could. Grasping a lighter, I moved into the clearing to duel with my massive, enraged foe.

The bear shifted its attention immediately to me, rearing on her hind legs to her massively full height. Could she really be almost ten feet tall? She roared with fury, paws clawing the ground and spittle glistening her jaws. The bear resumed her pounced stance, ready to charge. Her landing front paws shook the ground, almost causing my knees to buckle. She was ready to charge, her jaws open in anticipation. At that moment and holding the stick, I ignited the paraffin-soaked t-shirt with the lighter. It was our only hope of survival. The shirt blazed up with a powerful fireball blast. I thrust my makeshift torch forward, swaying it from side to side, the heat singeing my arm hairs and lightly cooking my fingers.

Perhaps out of shock or fear, the bear retreated, then bounded back in little skips as she assessed the possibility of two hearty meals, not one. But the intense fire threatened her and kept her at bay. Emboldened by my slight success, I began a roaring scream, hollering incoherently as loud as I could. Chihiro now appeared more scared by my ruckus than the bear, now confused and steadily retreating.

At this point, to our collective horror, Chihiro and I realised together that my torch was running out of fuel and dimming as quickly as it had blazed. It was now half the size it had been less than a minute before. As the forest seemed to close in on our private little drama, we watched the bear slow her retreat to a trickle, her tongue remoistening her open jaws. It dawned on me that nothing short of divine intervention or a trick of the devil could save us now.

Suddenly, another scream shook the forest. The bear swivelled around to find the source of the scream, no longer even mildly concerned about my torch's wilting fire. A second scream rang out, louder and infinitely more desperate before, and the bear charged away towards the sound, leaving a storm of dust in her wake.

Chihiro jumped down, staggering momentarily as she regained her balance. Her legs and arms were scarred with bloody scratches from ferociously clinging for her life to the tree truck and its branches.

'Are you OK?'

The look she gave me said more than a thousand words. It was a mixture of relief from surviving and rage from being put in that situation in the first place by no fault of her own. She picked herself up as I repacked my backpack. I threw the burned-out torch to the ground as it was now a mass of scorched wood and melted polyester-cotton material. We fled the scene towards the coast, jogging at a steady pace, neither of us mentioning Johnny, not even as a passing shrug to his well-being.

The trees thinned out both in mass and height as we got closer to the coast. Seagulls in the distance welcomed us. The sun blazed between the forest edge and the shore like a light at the end of a tunnel, and soon we could hear the shifting sea with its gently lapping waves. The forest's soft carpet floor of dead plant matter morphed into the beach's small, hard pebbles.

Chapter Twenty-Nine

The waves were smooth, their soft rolling showing no hint of storm or even mild tempest on the horizon. Only the shadow of a distant island outline interrupted the view – as though calling us. My attention was drawn to the tide now retreating at a fair pace. The forest was now in the distance, yet we needed to discuss one ugly matter.

'We have to go back for Johnny, or at least try and find help.'

'There is no help for miles. Look, do you see anyone? It's hours to walk to the nearest town, and there's no mobile phone signal.'

'So *we* go and look for him then?'

'Are you insane? We only just escaped this time. I doubt the bear has forgotten us. For all we know it could be tracking us now, stalking us in the shadows at the edge of the forest, ready to finish off what it started.'

'We can't just leave him,' I feebly protested.

'Why? He seems to bring all these problems on himself. The yakuza didn't cut off his little finger for sport. He should not even be here. He is turning this trip into a greater disaster by the hour. What idiot picks up a bear cub as though it's a cuddly toy? No sane person! Only someone who's so self-centred he thinks only of himself.'

It was hard to disagree with her, and I could understand her anger. I was angry at Johnny's stupidity, too. Yet leaving Johnny this way just didn't seem right. Her cold logic and apparent lack of basic humanity unnerved me.

Suddenly, we noticed a stirring at the edge of the distant forest. We feared it was the bear, but no. It was Johnny walking towards us. As he got closer, we could see that he had bloody specks on his face and forearms as thick as paint. His hands were covered in blood, almost dripping. His arms were a crisscross of light scratches and deep bite marks, all oozing his life force. When I saw his grey complexion, I had to wonder if I was witnessing his last moments of life. He moved past us without a touch of acknowledgement and walked into the sea, leaving a small slick of blood in his wake. We followed and watched as he gently washed the blood away as though in a trance.

'I see my plan worked. You both escaped the bear,' he stated in a far-off voice becoming stronger with every passing syllable.

Chihiro and I were confused. Apart from running away at full speed, any bear escape plan was news to us. My first instinctive conclusion was that the bear had found and attacked him, but I quickly dismissed such a notion. If that had happened, Johnny would be eviscerated and splayed over the forest floor, not cleaning himself off now. Yet the idea that he killed the bear in a one-on-one fight was too ludicrous to contemplate.

'After I realised the bear wasn't following me, I figured she had run after one of you instead. I snuck back to where we had been to try and follow her tracks and whichever unfortunate one of you she had picked out for dinner. Unfortunately, I'm no tracker. I found no obvious signs of where either of you had fled to or if the bear had accompanied you, and I knew there was no time for rough detection or guesswork as every moment wasted might bring you an inch closer to her jaws. I was in a panic till I saw the little beast who had brought on this calamity. A plan came to mind so quickly its vulgarity almost made me vomit with shame, but my lack of any other options was fuel, as always, for the devil's work.'

His mind seemed to stop and his voice became softer. His skin was now clean, but his clothes were a grim tie dye of different shades of ribboned blood encrusted in the fabric. A strong stench of fear and disgust radiated from his every pore. He waded out of the water back onto the beach, avoiding the coming guilty confession. I doubted it was going to relieve his conscience. He finally sat down as if the weight of events was too heavy to stand any longer. Like priests, Chihiro and I sat on each side of him, waiting for his confession.

'I sat the bear cub on a rock like a large obedient toddler. It made no effort to escape, just stared back, bored, innocent of the tragedy elicited by his mere presence. My plan was as simple as it was brutal. If I could get the bear cub to cry out in pain, its mother's maternal instinct would override her baseline bloodlust, causing her to return to her child and giving you both enough time to save yourselves. I figured I'd have time to make a run for it in the opposite direction. First, I slapped the cub across the face, but it didn't even blink, just licked its jaws a bit mockingly. Then I punched it, yet apart from almost toppling over, it didn't give a whisper of pain or protest. Again, it wet its jaws. I suspect I did more damage to my hand than to my target. Finally, I took out my pen knife and grabbed it by the throat, pinned it down and put the blade between its teeth. I started to surgically cut at the gums it had so enjoyed flaunting me with. As blood began dribbling down the blade, panic now filled its eyes. It started to struggle. As it panted in panic, I constricted my grip. To raise the volume of its cries, I began hacking away around the teeth, blood spraying and lumps of gums splattering. Its little feet thrashed away in thin air as it tried to escape. The sound was now a loud moan, but I needed it to evolve into a raging howl to carry the distance. So I flipped out the pliers on the pen knife, clenched it round one of the teeth and started to shake it lose. Instead, it snapped about two thirds down, splintering into dozens of fragments which slipped into the cub's throat, slicing it with each swallow. The cub finally cried out enough to startle me and shake the birds from the branches. But I knew its mother could be many miles away by now. I needed its wails to fill the whole valley. Although it was no doubt in pain, it still seemed to have little fear for its life. That was the catalyst I needed. It already had more than one chipped tooth, so it was time to cut away something unscarred and more indispensable. I placed the point of the blade against the corner skin folds of the left eye and slowly and gently ran it along the contours of the eye socket behind the eyeball. Now the howl I was waiting for began to build. With one motion, I pushed the knife down and pulled, scooping out the eyeball and hurtling it to the ground. Finally, I achieved the volume I needed. I did the same with the other eye, but now I took my time. Its begging howls grew in desperation. Just then, I heard the mother call out as she approached. In a frenzy, I stabbed the cub dozens of times to completely occupy her. Then I dashed away, finally finding my way back to you both.'

The barbarity of the act, despite its noble intent, seemed to pause the world for us. Sacrificing your own soul by maiming innocents, even to save others, is too high a price to pay. Chihiro and I were lost for words, and Johnny made it clear that the conversation was closed. I suspected that like so many near-misses in his life, he would lock this away, too, never to revisit it again or learn anything from it. Instead, he would likely transform the story into a funny Saturday-night anecdote, a twisted tale filled with totally justified actions. Johnny's lack of empathy for the bear cub was equal to Chihiro's scarce regard for Johnny's life. The absence of basic compassion in both appalled me deeply.

For now, though, we needed to put the bears behind us and take our next steps.

Chapter Thirty

'We need to find this ageless eye, whatever that is. We had better follow the coast to where the stream joins the sea,' Chihiro said, trying to focus our attention on anything apart from the horrors of the last few hours.

Together, we turned and walked briskly down the beach to try and outrun the past. We soon came to the stream we had been following before the bear intermission, cutting across the beach into the sea. We found nothing extraordinary in any direction apart from a scattering of large boulders and the standard beach coating of seashells, pebbles and sand.

As the day turned into evening, I suddenly realised that we would soon have another more savage problem to solve than our century-old Ainu poem riddle written on the canvas I had found.

'We can't camp here or anywhere else on the peninsula with a grief-stricken, psychotic bear roaming around looking for revenge. I really don't fancy waking up in the middle of the night to find myself half eaten. We will have to find this ageless eye, then walk to the nearest town, Rausu, and the safety of hotel walls, even if it means travelling through the night and returning to search tomorrow. As there are only a few hours of decent sunlight left, we need to proceed quickly. I suggest we split up but keep within sight of each other, find the trail of tears and hope the ageless eye – whatever it is – may still be nearby.'

Our first step was to find the stream we were following before our rude interruption from the bear attack broke our concentration, pushing us off course. We headed west up the beach, hoping we hadn't wasted too much time, scanning the tree line for any breaks and walking in silence. We looked everywhere except at each other's faces, as if our lack of acknowledgement would somehow heal or erase the last three hours. Luck was on our side for the first time that day. In less than an hour, even at our sluggish pace, we found the stream creeping out of the forest and shedding into the sea.

I headed up the beach while Chihiro studied the area. We were looking for the poem's "ageless eye" and decided to follow the river to where it joined the sea while Johnny wandered around absently. The coast curved west towards the stream we were originally following, the forest now behind us. We noticed how the ground suddenly arched up sharply and steeply into a cliff, rising just before the riverbank. We climbed up to the top of the cliff. Its bare rock had been blasted lifeless by the salt-laced wind. Thousands of tears sourced from multiple mountain waterfalls trickled down its face. We turned back towards the sea to follow the cliff's crest. In about a kilometre, the cliff bent sharply down to the beach before being swallowed into the surf.

We followed the cliff down to the beach again. I turned to watch the sea retreating and the sodden sand reclaim the high ground for the next few hours. After turning for a slow, concentrated panorama of the landscape, I was no nearer to the answer. We looked up and watched as Johnny slowly approached, hands in pockets, defeat radiating from his every step. I looked out into the setting sun, hoping for some form of inspiration, no matter how small, to help us on our way.

Beside us now, Johnny skimmed stones against the waves. He was lucky to get more the two skips. His gesture was futile, a perfect metaphor for our quest, hope for success dying with the fading light. Chihiro decided to recheck the area we had just investigated in one last desperate roll of the dice. Where was the "ageless eye", and what could it be? She ran to cover as much ground as possible and was nowhere nearer a solution when she returned.

'"Look through the ageless eye which is eaten by time" – maybe we are too late, maybe it has been moved or destroyed over the decades. Maybe time has eaten it completely and the treasures, whatever they may be, are long lost. The only chance of finding them now is pure blind luck, not enlightened deduction.'

As negative as her assessment was, no doubt it was more realistic than I wanted to admit. Our attention returned to Johnny, whose stone-skimming had improved as the sea thinned in its retreat. He had now managed to reach a lone rock outcrop curved like a sideways sickle blade and was trying to bounce the pebbles over the arch, which slowly emerged from the water. I held my hand to shield my eyes when the pieces finally fell into place.

I ran into the surf at full speed, but the knee-high water soon dragged me down to a fast walk. I ran my hands over the rocks' curves to find them unnaturally smooth, not by the rhythm of eroding water, but carved by people. Like a madman, I clawed in the water and pulled up one end of a large, arched stone, which I hoped would justify my mix of hypothesis and madness. I nodded to Johnny, who joined me on the other end. With one heavy heave, we pulled out half of the rock arch and placed it on the legs of the other submerged half to form a whole circle rising out of the water. Looking towards the sea horizon through the circle frame, I saw a distant island of dense green mountains hovering along its spine. I turned around towards the cliff Chihiro had just discovered. From our current position, the trickles covering the ridge looked like one solitarily gleaming waterfall.

'Quick! Stand with your back to the waterfall and look through the circle to find our destination on the island!' I shouted back to Chihiro as we struggled to keep the heavy rock balanced on its eroded perch.

Chihiro lined herself up with the map, and we were all in sync for a moment. But soon, our strength gave way, and, with a loud splash, the rock fell noisily back to its resting place. With our arms aching, we ran back to Chihiro to find that she had drawn the circle on our map. Chihiro pointed to one mountain that jutted much higher than the rest. It rested in the centre of the stone iris, jaggedly tearing the horizon with a glistening opal lake.

Chapter Thirty-One

Rausu is a town of less than 6,000 people. Most people in the town work as fishermen or tourist guides. A few local convenience stores and restaurants paper over the social cracks. There are three schools for a handful of pupils, their classes dwindling every year from youth emigrating to the bigger, brighter cities. The whole town has been withering for decades, and those left behind wait for the town's inevitable collapse.

We staggered into Rausu, ragged in pace and beleaguered in breath. We were high on the success of unriddling the Ainu clues but low from the carnage of the bear attack. Our limbs were wrung out to near collapse from covering just sixteen kilometres over twelve hours through wild, unkempt terrain.

We found a small diner called Matsuo Ramen. The morning's fresh catches deliciously filled all its dishes. Formerly the ground floor of a medium-sized house, the diner was now decked out in plastic wood and leather polymer and filled with local fishermen so used to their seats' curves they appeared moulded to them. The air was heavy with fish scent and wisps of smoke.

Midnight approached, and Chihiro pleaded with the manager to help us find rooms in town for the night. Something primitive had stirred us from our sole day in the wilds, alarming us all, so we hoped being in town would prevent us from going feral. Our host wrote a list of the few accommodations in town and eventually let Chihiro use his phone. There were only three hostels in town. By all accounts, their conversions from large houses had been made more out of financial necessity than anything else. They catered mainly to young backpackers and old sea fisherman. There was only one hostel – Okigaruya Hostel – that had rooms available. We trudged into the town centre up the one main road running parallel to the Rausu River. We passed a cluster of multicoloured concrete homes braced for earthquake blasts and flash flooding. The obligatory shrine was perched on a nearby hillside. Okigaruya Hostel was a characterless grey concrete block. It would be hard to imagine a more humourless building, but it offered beds and showers, so we stayed. After showering off the day's grime, we met to decide the details for our next stage of the plan.

Chihiro had been talking to a few locals and studying the hostel lobby's local tour guide pamphlet. Her frown told me we weren't going to like the results of her inquiries and research.

'We have a problem, a big problem. The island we need to get to, Kunashir, has been under Russian control since the end of World War II. There is no ferry or way of hiring a boat to cross the sea. The only way is to backtrack to Sapporo to get a plane, but the flights are once a week and go to the other end of the island. And I doubt we would get out of the only town there without raising suspicions as the place is hardly a tourist hotspot.'

'How far is the shortest distance between Hokkaidō and Kunashir?'

We studied the map and determined it was roughly twenty-five kilometres from shore to shore.

We now needed to find how heavily patrolled the sea lanes were and hope it was nowhere near as congested as the English Channel. We also needed to discover how we could acquire passage on a boat, legally or otherwise, as we wanted to slip across the following night. All this revolved in our heads as we dragged ourselves to our rooms to put the day's endless nightmare to rest.

The next day we decided I would go and look at the boats in the harbour, playing the naive tourist to see if a fisherman would sneak us over. Chihiro would see what she could find out about Kunashir Island from the locals. We left Johnny in his room, stinking of disinfectant, to fully recover from the bear cub mauling.

In my broken Japanese, and with the help of a few younger fishermen with their fractured English, I soon learnt that there was no chance they would take us to Kunashir Island. This was more out of shame of losing the island after World War II than for any practical reason; as they let slip, there were only Japanese fishermen working in that area. Russian vessels of any kind were unheard of as they congregate at the top of the island, and our southern destination was inhabited. The nearest settlement was almost forty kilometres midway up the island. I thanked them for their time, and they apologised for not being able to help more. I then made my way back to Okigaruya Hostel to see if Chihiro had had any more luck.

I found Johnny having a very late breakfast with a perplexed look clouding his face. For once, it was not because of the odd food he had ordered with his clumsy Japanese. He was looking over a paper with a level of concentration I had never seen before, and it took me a moment to understand what had hooked his focus so completely. I looked over his shoulder and saw a front-page photograph of Professor Haruto staring back at us, the expert we had met in Sapporo two days earlier. Bold banner letters screamed of his murder. I turned the page and was blitzed by a photo spread showing the professor as a young child in the bombed-out aftermath of World War II, then his plain, whitewashed high school, then his university graduation photo. Each one showed him growing in both height and intellectual pursuit, his brow becoming ever more serious by the passing decades. The next photo was a picture of him as a young researcher up to his knees in a muddy trench on some archaeological dig, holding up a piece of simple pottery. Finally, I saw his university professor photo. He was now in middle age and in full esteem. I was looking at a whole life mapped out in only five photographs, yet the ending was the truly extraordinary chapter. All the details of his life and death were in front of us in proud Japanese, which was Martian to Johnny and me.

'I can't read the rest, but this is dated the day after we left Sapporo. We need to find out more. You distract Chihiro this afternoon, and I will try and find someone to translate the article.'

Johnny hastily concealed the newspaper when Chihiro appeared around the corner to join us. She sat down and ordered lunch.

'Did you have any luck?'

'Not really. No one goes near the island unless for shelter if caught out by a storm. Going to satisfy our curiosity isn't a good enough excuse by a long shot, regardless of how much we pay them.'

'Can we hire a boat? We can say we want to take a trip around the coast or sail around the peninsula.'

'The town may be mostly for tourists, but the port is solely for fishing. I doubt even if we found a boat, they would let us hire it. We are hardly salty seamen with the skills to pilot a craft or the knowledge to convince them we do.'

'So we are going to have to borrow a boat for a few days?'

'That may be possible. There are many abandoned small boats at the harbour's far end well away from any streetlights or roads.'

'They may be abandoned for a good reason, but it's worth checking out. Otherwise, we're really out of options.'

'It's settled then. We'll go and see if there is anything near shipshape for our short voyage. I have some knowledge of boats due to various scuba diving trips, so we won't be going in completely blind. Johnny can stay and recover from his bear-inflicted injuries. We will have to bury our collective mental trauma for now.'

Chapter Thirty-Two

The far end of the harbour was like a boat scrapyard-cum-graveyard – just out of view and out of mind, around a steep curve that sharply fell towards the sea. It would be locked and dog-patrolled anywhere else in the world but Japan, where rural crime is rare. We saw scattered boats in every shade of the rainbow, survivors of a thousand storms and countless nautical miles. They all lay discarded like man-made coral, rotting back to nature's embrace as the sea mockingly laps at their keels.

With only the slightest inspection, we could see that the wooden boats were worthless. They had been devastated by rot and wood worm. The boat had to be large enough to carry the three of us and our supplies, and it had to be seaworthy enough to make the roundtrip journey without disintegrating around us. Lastly, it had to be fairly easy to sneak out. We had a shallow choice of craft for such a tall list of requirements and so little time.

We walked between the rotting and rusted wrecks, trying to look as casual as possible to any observers. That wasn't easy. At this boat cemetery, it was hard to pretend we were on some romantic walk or an unofficial history tour of past glories now shattered in the present. Still, it was a morbid boat show. The shale beach was littered with dead boats, from shells of large vessels, once floating homes, to small crafts hardly big enough to fit one average person. The shore was blighted by piles of bright orange, frayed fishing nets and pierced sea buoys, their plastic shells thick with moss and tangled with driftwood. It was also littered with steel barrels corroded to oxide red, their bleeding oil leaving the pebbles below a cancerous black. A film of nautical pollution sprawled in disarray over the beach's edge.

'Can you see anything useful and travel-worthy? You're the expert, after all,' Chihiro asked.

'I never claimed to be an expert, just vaguely competent. But even a city dweller who has never seen a boat or the sea before in their life could tell these are all wrecks. I'll have a good look around and see what I can find.'

I walked around the wrecks to find them stripped bare by scavengers who had picked them apart with expert Japanese proficiency. Many were now just brittle skeleton frames, their compartments long caved in, their sides collapsed. The only things left were steel and wooden-hulled boats, many decades out of date, constructed long before plastic came into use – the only commodity sea salt can't rust. All hope had deserted me when, in the far corner and half-covered in debris, I saw a yellow shell peeking out.

It was a small, open lifeboat, roughly five metres by two metres. It had been used as a supply boat or, in desperate circumstances, as an emergency escape raft from a larger ship. It was now moss-riddled, and a pool of rainwater doubling as a pond for local insects was a testament that the rubber rim was most likely watertight. I gently placed my foot on its front and rocked it to gauge its weight. The boat was definitely light enough for hauling and paddling. I found no holes or gouges below the would-be waterline, so I picked it up and placed it upside down on the dock to drain. While I was inspecting it, Chihiro appeared from behind a rusted barge. When she saw my discovery, a distinctly unimpressed look clouded her face.

'Is this really the best you can find?'

'Unless you had any more luck and can do better, yes. Trust me, I have no desire to meet Davy Jones anytime soon either. We'll need some paddles and a compass bearing before we set off to avoid getting lost and disoriented in the dark in the middle of the sea and landing back on the peninsula down the coast.'

I looked over at Kunashir Island simmering in the distance. Its peaks were hidden in mist, its shores filled with reflected light. There were only a few fishing boats sitting in the sea, harvesting fish in the darkness of night. I reckoned it should not be too hard to sneak by unobserved. We returned to town to find some paddles and figure out our best departure time to avoid the fishing boat rush-hour traffic.

In Rausu, we split up. Chihiro went to find some paddles and information on fishing boat schedules. Our cover story was that we had planned to go sea fishing in an inflatable raft and had forgotten the paddles in Tokyo. I hoped she could spin that ludicrous tale at least slightly convincingly. My job was to find Johnny, see if he had recovered, and update him on our progress. Chihiro didn't try to hide her hope that Johnny would drop out or at least stay behind as she considered him a hindrance and dangerous liability. Yet I knew that with his obligations to the yakuza, for him, it was now either success or death. There was no middle road.

Chapter Thirty-Three

I found Johnny in his room, the same unhinged mourning look now carved deeper into his face. Next to the newspaper, there was a Japanese notepad with pages that turned left to right – the opposite of Europe (and, incidentally, most of the world). He had written a series of poorly scribbled bullet points on one page, the feeble lettering no doubt due to his still-savaged limbs and frenzied state.

'I finally managed to find someone with above-basic English to translate the article. The gist of the story is that the professor's body was found two days ago. According to the coroner, he was murdered the night after our visit, or maybe the morning after. What's more, witnesses saw two Western males and one Japanese female leaving his property around the afternoon before the killing. The police are now looking for us for questioning.'

I was stunned. I fell into a chair, my mind too muddled to find any direction or possible solution. I knew that one of my companions had to be the murderer, and both had their reasons. Neither had the shame or guilt required to admit their crime.

'Chihiro is a murderer. She poisoned us both. Then, when we were bedridden, she slipped out and killed the professor.

Then she snuck back here, hoping to use our intoxicated condition as an alibi. Do you think she's going to let a little thing like morals and scruples get in her way of solely having the glory? I saw her lack of concern for my injuries. She didn't even bat an eyelid or hesitate for a moment to push on after our sick-fest in Tokyo. Think about it. She hasn't mentioned the murder, despite the fact she must have seen the newspapers by now or at least a television bulletin in passing. If we are pulled up by the police – remembering she's a Japanese woman and we're foreign males – we'll be charged, tried and imprisoned before we can get a word out in our defence. Remember what they said at induction? There is no concept of European habeas corpus in the Land of the Rising Sun.'

'We can't raise her suspicions. We still need her on the island. Keep a close eye on her when we get there, and as soon as we return, we'll wait for the perfect moment to ditch her. Then we'll make a run straight for the airport, call the yakuza to meet us there, give them the statues, and leave the country as soon as possible.'

It was a wafer-thin plan, but it was all I could drum up in the heat of the moment. It seemed to settle Johnny's mind, and he gave a nod in agreement. We threw out the newspaper and notes, then set out to meet Chihiro to see if she had managed to acquire the paddles.

We now sat on the beach waiting for Chihiro. Finally, she returned with a pair of paddles and information in hand. All the pieces were ready for finalising our plan.

'The fishing boats leave just after dark and retire at first light. That will give us a five-hour window. All twenty boats leave at around the same time, and it takes just over an hour, so if we give them an hour's headway, they should be gone when we leave. The boats go to the more fertile and deeper fishing waters at the bottom of Kunashir Island or at the top of Shiretoko Peninsula. This will leave our route relatively clear.'

'What's tonight's weather?'

'It should be fine for the next three days, giving us enough time to get there, find the treasure and get back. But there's a low-pressure front coming, which would really be best to avoid. We don't want to get trapped on the island. Paddling back even in just a light storm would be suicidal.'

'So we leave tonight. All the stores are closed now, but we should have just enough food to last us for the trip. I suggest we pack, then get some sleep. I will pay for our rooms and meet you by the boat at midnight. I suggest we go there separately to avoid raising too much suspicion.'

Chihiro looked around to see if Johnny or I had anything more to add to the discussion. We answered with blank stares. We returned to our respective rooms to rest. After a few hours of heavy sleep, I was rudely (and dramatically) awakened by a very feminine hand over my mouth, the other silently motioning me outside, leaving Johnny happily snoring away.

In the still night air and starry sky, a light wind stirred around us. A frantic Chihiro smoothed out a familiar-looking newspaper and a badly scribbled set of bullet points.

'I found this in your room when I checked up on Johnny this afternoon. He was also acting more suspiciously than normal. It's a newspaper from Sapporo. The professor was murdered in the early morning after our visit! He was beaten to death with a statue from his mantelpiece. Johnny's notes suggest that I did it, but how can that be true? I was in bed ill all night – as were you. Johnny must have snuck out while we were both incapacitated!'

Déjà vu is an annoyance at the best of times, but when faced with a murder in your midst, it's devastatingly inconvenient.

This is even more true when you're about to set off on a voyage and need all on board. I was now looking at potential assassins to help me in my quest. One because she was the only person who could read the language, the other because he had the muscle to pull on the oars to get to our destination in the shortest time possible. This was not good.

'The best we can do is not to raise his suspicion. We still need him to get to the island. Keep a close eye on him, and when we get there and as soon as we return, we wait for the perfect moment to ditch him and make a run straight back to the police in Sapporo.'

It was almost exactly the same word-for-word speech I had given Johnny earlier in the day. Chihiro's answer was cut short when Johnny, awake now, joined us outside. Seeing him, she vanished back into her room to meet us at the boat in an hour's time. She left me shivering in the night next to Johnny.

I was now caught between reasonable paranoia about my companion's intentions and the naive forlorn hope that the murder was all an unhappy coincidence. Yet it didn't matter now. I had passed the point of no return in a far-flung corner of a foreign land, an alien to its language and customs. The only hope for my safety was their need for each other for the next few days and that their mutual suspicions would act as a perverted form of equilibrium that would hold till we returned to Hokkaidō.

Chapter Thirty-Four

The other guests of the Okigaruya Hostel had long gone to bed when I crept out into the night and began walking down the main street. Winking lights peeked out into the night's blackness from a few homes, but most were dark. The streets were empty. My only serenade was the scurrying meow of the occasional cat and the anxious barks of distant dogs. The three of us met by the boat I had picked out. I checked and confirmed the harbour was deserted. The twinkling stars were the only lights in the harbour to chaperone us. It was time to go.

Johnny and I picked up the boat and gently walked it into the shallows. The bitter-cold water bit at our ankles. Johnny held the boat still while Chihiro and I filled it with our supplies, trying our best to space the weight evenly in the muted light. I had taken a compass bearing off the map and lined up our boat roughly in the right direction. We put on our life jackets. Chihiro climbed in and sat crossed-legged at the front of the boat to navigate with the compass while Johnny and I sat in the back at either side like a two-stroke engine. We quietly pushed against the shallow floor, the boat rocking violently as we unhelpfully zig-zagged away from shore into the sea. Eventually, we got the strength and rhythm of our strokes in tandem. We steadily moved forward at a slow but steady pace, our speed increasing with our confidence.

The shore slipped away, and the town's remaining lights dimmed. The splash of our oars dipping into the sea and our heavy, labour-stretched breathing were the only sounds we could hear. Chihiro grasped the compass in one hand while directing with the other. However, soon she was forced to resign from these roles for violent and loud vomiting, seasick to the core. She stretched her head over the boat edge and regurgitated everything into the sea, much to Johnny's poorly hidden amusement.

In the darkness, it was hard to work out how much progress we were making. The growing silhouette of our island destination, its mountains rising menacingly upward and drowning out the stars, hinted we were on track. By now we had mastered a steady pace without too much rocking. Still, Chihiro could not seem to control her seasickness even though her stomach was now quite empty. Yet in her solitude at the front of the boat, away from our continuous splashing, her senses remained unclouded.

Chihiro's hand shot up and spun around to shush us. We stopped paddling. All we could hear was the sound of waves hitting the side of our boat. At first, I wondered if her seasickness had made her delirious. Then I heard what had earned her vomit-frayed attention.

Chapter Thirty-Five

We heard Japanese voices, their dialect lazy in delivery. In the night's stillness, it was hard to gauge how far or near they were. It took a few moments of frantic searching till Johnny found the source. He thrashed the air with his outstretched finger in their direction.

It was a boat sitting to our left. It was hard to know how far away they were as the darkness made an accurate estimate almost impossible. The craft could be anything from a small recreational fishing boat to a large trawler, but at the moment it was just a dark mass. Its only giveaway was the starlight covering its slowly approaching bulk. Alarmingly, the sea currents were slowly but resolutely pushing us towards the voices, their chatter growing louder each moment.

It is hard to communicate in silence and almost impossible in total darkness. Add to that the fact we were in a "stolen" boat, on a foreign sea, miles from land, and on what many would consider an illegal voyage – well, the situation appeared very bleak to the three of us.

First, we had to determine the distance between us and the incoming boat. Second, we had to see if it was possible to sneak past them. In unison, we peered into the darkness, each momentary snip of conversation helping us to home in on our target.

It was a large boat. As we watched, it cut its shape into the sky, covering more stars by the moment. A dim halo of light grew as we got closer. Now it was clear the boat was heading in our direction at a slow speed. With only moments to spare, we huddled in the middle of our little boat to decide on our strategy.

'What do we do? We can't just paddle past; we would make too much noise. But we can't just sit here – if it hits us, we will be smashed to smithereens,' Chihiro whispered urgently.

Johnny looked more dumbstruck than usual. His solo contribution was a weary shrug, leaving everything to me. I thought about things for a moment, then grasped onto a plan.

'With the sea current, I think I can steer us past using a paddle like a rudder at the back of a ship. You two will have to gently push us away from the fishing boat if we get too close. I will sit at the back and you both need to be on the right side. It's only a medium-sized ship, and it's moving slowly, so there is little chance of us getting sucked under in its wake. Their deck is high enough so any casual glances should overshoot us.'

The boat was bearing down on us and there was no time for discussion. We took our places, sliding our supplies as counterweights as we took our new positions. The front tip of the fishing boat sliced the water a mere ten feet in front of us as I slipped the paddle in and pulled a hard right. Our boat lurched violently, causing a jutting bob and throwing us all off balance. The fishing boat began a silent slide past us, but it soon pulled us back into its dominating orbit like a blazing comet passing a lonely asteroid. Johnny and Chihiro steadied themselves as best they could, stretching out their arms to push against the fishing boat's hull if necessary.

Suddenly, a high-force blast of water shooting between the ships' hulls showered us with freezing, piercing ice fingers. The momentum was so great it sent Chihiro crashing to the bottom of the boat, almost unseating Johnny, who pushed with all his might, barely saving us from disaster. They got back into position as we silently ricocheted off the hull. Soon we got into a rhythm – them pushing off, me pulling away. Finally, with one last great push, we broke orbit and catapulted out of the fishing boat's sphere of influence.

We all sat there in silence, panting, watching as the fishing boat went on its way, oblivious to our crisis. After it had moved to a safe distance, we resumed our original positions in the boat. Thankfully, the compass indicated that we hadn't gone too far off course. We quickly moved forward, hoping there would be no more boats or other unfortunate events in our way as we raced against a rapidly rising dawn that would spotlight our folly to the world if we didn't get out of its way.

Part Four

Chapter Thirty-Six

Kunashir Island hung on the horizon as dawn swept away the night's shadows. Each weary pull of the oars sluggishly cut the surf till, mercifully, the sea waves began pushing us towards the shore, perhaps out of pity for our own feeble efforts, showing mercy to our aching arms and burning shoulders. Unfortunately, when we ceased rowing, our limbs quickly froze. We had to swap relief from muscle aches and pains for cold shivers as the wind whipped us with cutting, salty teeth. As the morning sun's rays on the shore revealed large rocks reaching out from the pebbles carpeting the beach, the screams of morning seagulls, fighting to be heard over the abrasive slosh of the shallowing sea, filled the air.

Apart from the seagulls, we had no company on the beach or the nearby sea. We hoped our good luck would last at least the morning, at a stretch the whole day, if there was any justice in the world. I could see the sea floor under increasingly shallow waves as we advanced the final push to the shore, Johnny heaving on the oars, Chihiro and me at each side at the front on the lookout for any large rocks that could rip the hull, leaving us stranded Robinson Crusoe-style.

When we were near enough to the shore, I jumped into the shallows to pull on the tug line and steer us along the shortest path possible to the shore. Johnny pushed from the back while Chihiro crouched in the middle for ballast, tottering awkwardly with each pull and push. Finally, we reached the shore and hauled out the boat. I collapsed, every muscle burning. Johnny, staggering, sat down beside me. Chihiro stumbled up the beach as though drunk, her fresh sea legs protesting the return to land. The whirlpool of seasickness had weakened her. She sat down on my other side. We laid there in a ten-minute silence, recharging our facilities and reawakening our reasons for being where we were. For the first time on this strange journey, we were on equal footing in habitat and cultural surroundings: we were all interlopers.

As our exhaustion waned, an anxious worry reawakened our sense of caution: no doubt about it, we could be discovered any minute. Like a bright orange flare nestling on the beach, our boat was a beacon for unwanted attention and enquiries. We searched the beach to find a hiding spot with enough foliage to pull over and camouflage it. We fanned out and searched the beach edge, finding dense grass and shallow, stunted trees. At last, Johnny found a ditch just deep enough to hold the boat. Using some rope, we tied handfuls of tree branches together, then wove the bunches into a thin green dome. We then left a small, unassuming pile of stones at the grass edge to mark the place of camouflage.

We split our camping supplies between two rucksacks, one for me, the other for Johnny, leaving Chihiro to cope with her seasick-drenched self and to prove that even in the most desperate of circumstances, chivalry was still not quite dead. Being slightly smaller and lighter than myself, Johnny carried the sleeping bags, our clothes, half the food, tent pegs and head torches. I took the rest of the food, cooking utensils and the tent canvas and poles, leaving no room for my Ainu book, which Chihiro squeezed into her camera bag.

From the beach, we headed up the valley, passing from white sand to thin grass and scrubland bush in a few steps. The trees grew thicker and higher as we followed the crease in the valley floor towards the nearest tallest mountain peak, hoping to plot our course to our final goal mountain with a lake at Kunashir's northern tip. That valley was so remote it was nameless on our map, just a scrunch of contour lines.

We stopped for lunch at a nearby, fast-running valley stream we used as our personal water cooler. The dense trees were our parasol, the breeze racing through the valley our air-conditioning. Our stiffness from the cramped boat journey and its back-breaking rowing had slowly receded, as had the painful muscle cramps. We had not properly rested since setting off just after midnight, and the day before we spent preparing for the trip. It dawned on us we been awake almost twenty-four hours straight.

Only now, when I was fully fed and mostly awake, I noticed just how curious the wildlife was. Brigades of chipmunks scaled trees, plucking their bounties, while a pair of sables sat at our feet, waiting to be fed or entertained. Instead of running around the forest as their mainland cousins did, the wildlife here simply sat and watched – foxes from their grass chairs or Blakiston's fish owls from their tree perches. As we cut our path through the virgin landscape, continuing our ascent from the green of the valley floor to the shale of the mountainside, it occurred to me that perhaps we were the first visitors here for centuries.

Chapter Thirty-Seven

From that vantage point, we could see the lake – our quest's final destination. It appeared as a softly glistening speck in the distant afternoon sun, just over eleven kilometres away as the crow flies. The question was how to get there: through the mountains or by the coast? The coast looked too inaccessible, requiring us to walk around a succession of almost vertical cliff faces rolling up and down the shore like the curves on ECG monitors. Such a trek would need specialist equipment and skills, not to mention time, that we did not process. Instead, we chose the high path. Between us and our final goal were layers of dense forest riding on the backs of jagged mountain ridges. We would have to hop from ridge to ridge to keep our bearings and lake in sight so as not to pass or overshoot it. A detailed map of the island would have helped, but that wasn't in the cards. We were now in the ruleless realm of pure wilderness with no footpaths or roads to aid our uninitiated selves, unable to read nature. To us, it was all just a nameless expanse. At least, that was true for the west side of the island.

Looking down from the peak to the east, we could see a one-lane dirt track running between the coast and the mountain ridges. The track's origin was the town of Yuzhno-

Kurilsk, the only real settlement on the island of just over 6,000 Russian fishermen and their families. That meant 6,000 pairs of eyes we had to avoid at all costs. Most of the town sat by the Furukamappu Bay on the northeast coast. We could also see a few smaller villages scattered along the northwest coast for twenty-two kilometres. This coastline led to our final destination: a tall mountain crowned with a lake. Lesser peaks, separated by crescent valleys and hills, crowded around the mountain. The vista greeted us like a pathless, giant, irregular hopscotch board we would traverse for the next few days. We figured that as long as we kept the mountains between the locals and us and were careful, we'd be able to avoid any curious eyes.

Around midday, after a small, dehydrated lunch of lukewarm noodles pots with saturated vegetables, we started our trek to the lake and (hopefully) its treasures. The rough terrain varied from one hour to the next. First, we scrambled up a mountainside of loose shale piles that slipped underfoot with the slightest of pressure. This cut our progress in half. We also had to feel our way with makeshift walking sticks through one valley's vast bog area, where one misplaced foot might mean the bog sucked off its walking boot with a gurgling gulp. Another time, windswept peaks barren of any shelter almost blew us into frighteningly deep crevasses.

We kept as high as possible as we moved from one mountain peak to another, keeping our distant goal in sight whenever possible. As the long hours passed, the lake grew nearer. Even so, it was soon clear it was going to take two days for us to get there. Our limbs were still tired from our previous land-and sea-based expeditions, and they ached more with each mile. Our backpack straps had chafed our shoulders near bloody, and our feet blisters had turned our socks a sodden crimson. As a rising wind heavy with nimbostratus clouds darkened the day to a close, we urgently looked for a suitable campsite.

It soon became apparent this part of our journey was going to be trickier than first anticipated. We didn't want to camp on a peak as we would be fully exposed to the incoming barrage of the elements, all definitely capable of tearing our flimsy nylon shelter to shreds in short order. The valley we had just trudged through was either damp or sodden with leg-consuming bogs. Waking up to find ourselves buried alive wasn't appealing to us. We had to find a happy medium quickly because the darkening sky hid more ground by the moment. In the creeping shadows, we finally settled on a relatively flat ledge in a protected area halfway down the mountainside – a dry plateau on the edge of the valley bogland. It was surrounded by shallow turf, just deep enough to hold our tent pegs. While we worked, lightning flashes in the distance interfered with our night eyes at the most inopportune moments, usually when a hammer was descending towards a peg, hitting hand or foot instead. The rain and wind began pounding just as we finished tying off the guy lines. Exhausted, we all fell into the tent in a bundle, zipping out the weather behind us. The mountainside sheltered us from the worst of the wind, leaving only the unrelenting rain to drum us to sleep after our hastily heated supper.

Chapter Thirty-Eight

At first, I thought I was dreaming about the strange noise in my light sleep, which was already heavily laced with swirling paranoia over a murder. Whatever it was seemed to be moving around inches away from me in the stifling humidity of our temporary home. Despite my best efforts to ignore the noise, it grew more distinct and louder between the thunder blasts. I finally gave in to curiosity and rolled over, forcing my eyes open.

On the tent's side, the lightning shadowed a massive silhouette of pointed ears and low jawline for just a moment. Instantly, I knew it was not the bear we had so savagely wronged, tracking us for its justified revenge. No. It was another predator just as dangerous, historically lethal in these parts. I listened. Its rhythmic panting echoed around me, now almost deafening. A startled Chihiro flew awake, displeased more than anything, not yet seeing what I saw.

'Wolf,' I softly hissed, as if the Canis lupus would hear me and begin its murderous attack.

Chihiro sighed and rolled her eyes. I had to admire her ability to show disdainful contempt in such dangerous circumstances.

'There are no wolves left in Japan or the surrounding islands anymore. They were hunted to extinction almost one hundred years ago, and they were only—'

A loud bark broke her condescending lecture, shock-waking Johnny in an instant and freezing us all with dread. The shadow had now shrunk as the lighting strikes grew more frequent, their thunderous afterbirth momentarily drowning out the canine's rapid panting. Johnny quickly unzipped the tent door to confront our very unwanted guest while I clutched a knife, ready to strike first if the mutt gave off the slightest sign of attack.

We were confronted by a beast as docile as a puppy. It hastily retreated from the noise when Johnny unzipped the tent's door. This would have been comfortingly cute, verging on adorable, if we hadn't noticed that its collar's nametag was in Cyrillic script, mockingly waving back at us. We held our breaths, waiting for someone else to speak. We feared that our discovery was imminent and didn't know how to avoid capture. Mere hours away from our goal, a cold Russian jail cell fate threatened us.

'We have to kill it quick, hide the body, and move on now before we are discovered,' Johnny the Bear-Cub-Torturer-Extraordinaire instructed. He pointed at my knife, hinting that the "we" really meant me.

'No. That will only draw attention when the dog vanishes, and if the corpse is found, it goes without saying the situation will deteriorate rapidly. But you're right, we do need to move now before—'

Numerous explosive bangs now echoed in the mountains above us, cutting off Chihiro. Unlike the long roars of thunder, these were short and sharp, easily recognised (from TV shows to video games) as gunshots. Maybe the shooters wanted to get our unwanted guest's attention. In any case, now we figured the dog was attached to the hunters. Our only consolation was knowing the gunshots, coming from the valley below, were presently faint, distant echoes. We hoped we were out of their sights, at least for now.

'I say we ditch the tent and head down to the coast as I can't see there being a reason for them to hunt there. Most of the game must be in the forest area of the mountains.'

I had no way of knowing if any of that statement was remotely true or accurate as I didn't know anything about hunting. Yet it clearly made sense to my companions, who agreed. We quickly exited the tent, sending the dog bounding into the night. Still, it's loud panting in the near distance revealed it hadn't abandoned us completely.

Johnny and I tore down the tent, wrapping it tightly with the guy lines before pile-driving it into the nearby bog, which greedily gulped it down. Meanwhile, Chihiro threw rocks into the darkness towards the unsettling panting to discourage our unwanted guest. On her third throw, a high-pitched whale indicated a bullseye, and we heard the crash of a dog running away down the mountain. As we couldn't use torches for fear of being spotted, we set off down the mountain's west side and headed to the coast with only lightning flashes for illumination as we were bombarded by thunder.

The long, unkempt and soaked grass was like slippery ice, causing more free-fall staggers then safe running. Rugged tree roots snatched spitefully at my ankles, causing me to trip and fall more then make any real progress. The rain, relentless, kept battering me down. I had to plan and memorise the route for the next dozen metres, adjusting my pace in the few microseconds of lightning strikes before darkness kicked back in. Chihiro and Johnny tumbled down the mountain in the same fashion.

At the bottom, the terrain flattened out. The trees also thinned out and withered while rough mountain rock changed to stone underfoot. As we walked, we had a direct view of the sea, its churning roars replacing the thunderstorm's bellows. Then we came to a vertical cliff drop, which we all very near toppled over, stopping just in time.

I turned to look back where we had come from, hoping to find that we had lost our pursuers, led on by their dogs' loud and threatening howls. I was disappointed. A faint flash of lighting backlit three silhouettes no more than a quarter of a kilometre away up the valley, the screeching dogs leading them on the wind. Johnny pointed, urging us to follow the coast. Knowing of no other options, we followed apprehensively as early dawn filtered over the horizon in the east. Like nocturnal animals, we would have to find a place to go to ground and wait for the threat to pass us by, saving us for another day.

We stooped low as we scuttled along the cliff, its edge leading to a sheer drop hundreds of feet down to the beach. To our left, the waves at the bottom of the cliff were gently breaking on the shore as though laughing at us. The recent storm's fury had now largely blown itself out, shuddering into calmness. Unfortunately, it was too light now to cut back into the forest depths and use its dense web of shadows for camouflage. The hunters were on flat ground now and would definitely see us. I was about to suggest looking for a way to scramble down the cliffs when a natural doorway, jagged and as dark as an abyss, caught my eye. I motioned to my companions and led the charge into the dark depths of the cave.

The cave's recessed gloom seemed infinite, yet my outstretched arms colliding into walls and bouncing off stalagmites soon broke that illusion. It was so heavy and dank in the cave that my eyes watered and my lungs tightened. I imagined that the dripping water was shimmering with unseen creepy-crawlies of the multi-legged and poisonous kind commonly found in such Japanese best-left-undisturbed hideaways.

When we got to the very edge of the light from the entrance, Chihiro produced a torch from her backpack, but its thin beam was soon lost in the darkness ahead. My spirits lifted, thinking there might be an exit out the other side. The subsiding storm let in the howling of the barking dogs behind us. The hunters were either officially on our trail or graced with uncanny intuition. As we moved forward, the cave slowly closed in, making us feel a bit claustrophobic. The cave became increasingly cold and clammy, its bleached moss walls showing no hint of life. Our anxious breaths may have been the only warmth felt there for eons. I was now so disoriented, I started to wonder if we were climbing to fresh-air freedom or walking into a private mass grave. I was debating how to bring such a tricky subject up when the corridor opened into a chamber. A quick flash of Chihiro's torch beam around the area revealed only one exit: the entrance we were standing in.

We stood there, stunned. Pools of gritty water rippled on the floor. Chihiro and Johnny began moving around the room and tapping on the wall as though hoping to find a hidden button or lost stone to push to open a secret passage to another chamber. The muffled echo of barking mixed with faint gobbledegook chatters, which I assumed to be Russian, steadily grew louder as they approached the cave mouth. Chihiro and Johnny picked up the pace of their frantic wall slapping despite knowing such action was unlikely to turn up anything. Meanwhile, I examined the ceiling, trying to think of a way to talk us out of getting arrested to avoid spending god knows how long in a modern Russian gulag. That was when I could have sworn I saw a shadow flickering back at me. Desperate to try just about anything, I leapt up to grab it.

My hand disappeared into the familiar feeling of dirt as I grabbed hold of what I assumed was a damp tree root. With one hard yank, half the ceiling began swaying, showering me in a cascade of soil. I grabbed the root with both hands and leant back with all my weight. Johnny now broke out of his trance and jumped up to join me. With our feet square against the cave sides, we pulled back with all our might, and a crisscross web of roots erupted across the ceiling. While Chihiro watched, a dam seemed to bust, sending Johnny and me to the cave floor in our personal dirt avalanche. The soil buried us waist deep as the unearthed morning sun above spread its rays on our dirt-filled eyes.

Panting, I climbed out of the dirt avalanche. My first greeting was blinding sunlight illuminating the freshly hollowed-out shaft Johnny and I had made in the roof. I grimaced as fresh air bellowed leftover dust into my eyes. Chihiro had crawled halfway up the six-foot shaft, and Johnny was getting ready to do the same. I couldn't help but notice that neither spared a moment to think of helping me. After throwing my bag over my shoulder, I started climbing after Johnny, squeezing and contorting with every pull to freedom. Alarmingly, we heard Russian voices trying to calm panicked dogs as they came closer. The sound of their voices fussing and comforting their dogs' barking blitz muffled our frantic scrambling, covering our escape.

The welcoming fresh air knocked the dank stink of the cave out of us. The howling dogs and their masters' chatter echoed through the shaft below, blending and sounding like unintelligible diabolic babble. There was no time to inspect our fresh cuts and darkening bruises from the climb. We hurriedly slipped away, heading to our final mountain top destination less than three hours away. Its lake, shimmering in the morning sun, called us on.

Chapter Thirty-Nine

We finally reached the lake at the bottom of the final peak, casting mid-afternoon shadows over us. The sulphur fumes rising off the volcanic lake teared up our eyes and assaulted our noses. Hovering over us from its slate-aged throne by at least 500 feet, the mountain peak watched the lake's ripples and a splatting of wafer-thin, shallow-rooted shrubs and grasses rebelliously clutching onto life. The shoreline around the lake was as lifeless and desolated as a moon crater. A rim of carpet-thin green weakly sprouted about three metres from the shore like a soft halo holding in the lake's sulphurous poison. Opposite us, just over a quarter of a kilometre away, sat a smaller, thinly stubbled hill. We dipped back down the peak to a fume-free slate rock overhang. Chihiro checked for poisonous insects. She hunted in holes for the bright, yellow-skinned Japanese keelback snake, then flipped over stones searching for the blood-red shell of the Mukade centipede. We made ourselves as comfortable as possible with layered slate as our mattress and speckled mould for wallpaper. Out of sight and downwind of the suffocating volcanic fumes, we laid down to rest for the night, our clothes stuffed underneath as a makeshift mattress. Sleep came quickly despite the tomb-like feel of our resting place.

I had made the schoolboy error of sleeping facing east. The rising sun is nature's alarm clock, and it rose early on this cloudless sky. Chihiro, sleeping beside me, could have acted like a human curtain for me, but her sleeping space was empty and her body warmth had long evaporated. With no clouds to ease the sun's spear-like glow, there was no way to return to any meaningful sleep, so I grudgingly got up. While walking a few feet out of sight to urinate, it occurred to me I didn't have to make such an effort as there were only two people in my immediate vicinity. That brought an ironic smile to my face.

I decided to leave Johnny happily snoring as it appeared he found peace only in sleep. In the waking world, the weight of his actions was suffocating him with fake remorse and blades of despair. Intuiting where Chihiro would be, I made the short walk up a modest hill and found her there, perched on a rock overlooking the lake and peak. With one hand, she was drying her hair with a towel. She was holding binoculars with the other while intently surveying the surroundings and mumbling to herself.

'We have to be quick. The Russians may reappear at any time, and we can get by with only so much luck and clever ruses. I suspect we are rapidly reaching our quota. "Find the island that appears purely by its own whim. All life is caught between the devil and the dusk".'

She absently repeated the last two clues over and over, still oblivious to my presence. The lake, rippling below, was the only large body of water on the island. It was the starting place for the final act of our play entitled *Between the Devil and the Dusk*, but as the water was bubbling and spewing sulphur, I didn't want to get too close. I preferred to investigate from afar.

'Maybe in Ainu times the lake was still normal and not volcanic?' I suggested, rather unhelpfully.

Chihiro, startled, looked over at me. 'No, they have been volcanic for tens of thousands of years. If anything, they've cooled over the centuries, leaving the current state of lukewarm water. The lakes must represent the devil, the dusk nightfall, but this information's useless without working out how an island can appear "by its own whim".'

Chihiro sighed heavily in defeat. Then, without a word or casual glance, she rose from her rock seat and trod past me, heading back to camp and leaving me to follow.

When we returned to camp, Johnny was up. The look of unnerving vacancy in his eyes grew stronger with each passing day. The threat of yakuza wrath was always present. Still, he had managed to ready the camping stove. We found him debating over which packet of cheap and tasteless dehydrated noodles to cook.

'We only have three days of food at most, four if we start rationing at half portions, seeing as we didn't have the time to buy more before we set off from Rausu.'

Since our lack of preparation was the gap-toothed fisherman's fault, not ours, Johnny's implied accusation fell flat.

'The lake is not that big and there are three of us, so we should be able to cover it easily in a few hours, never mind three days. A bit of optimism goes a long way, you know,' Chihiro stated cryptically.

We sat down to eat, our breakfast silence broken only by our slurping of lukewarm noodles.

Chapter Forty

We walked around the lake edge, first alone, then as a trio. Each time, we repeated the same lines to ourselves: 'Find the island that appears purely by its own whim,' and, 'All life is caught between the devil and the dusk.' The lake was roughly one kilometre long, moulded in a deformed, teardrop shape. There was nothing exceptional on the lake bank. There weren't any obvious signs of recent human struggle and strife. The only paths were animal tracks in the waist-high grass that receded at the lake's edge, the only constructions were bird nests decorating the branches of small trees. There were no human sounds apart from our own footsteps and laboured breathing. We were truly an alien element in the local ecosystem, something getting rarer in the world with every passing moment.

It was late afternoon by the time we had circumnavigated both lakes for the second time. The sun was slowly descending to the horizon, and we were no nearer to our goal. We had no idea of how to proceed. The only positive to be taken from the day was the lack of interference from any other human. Gratefully, we had not seen another soul, only the odd fishing boat in the distance. That was the only evidence that we were not alone in the world. We looked westward from the small lake back over the sea towards Shiretoko Peninsula and Rausu Harbour. After all this, would we return empty-handed?

'"...Find the island that appears purely by its own whim. All life is caught between the devil and the dusk." It's nonsense, isn't it?' I asked, like many times previously that day.

I watched a bird land on a rock by the lakeshore. The rock rose against the horizon of the lake's edge before disappearing under the water's waves, only to remerge freshly christened a moment later in a never-ending dance.

'Tidal island,' I whispered.

'What?'

'I visited Saint Michael's Mount in Cornwall when I was a child – an island that appears purely by its own whim. You can walk there, but only when the tide is low. That has to be it!'

We all turned towards the lake, the sun as its backdrop, its golden rays caressing the glittering waves.

'Do you get tidal islands in lakes?'

'Not that I know of. They're usually too shallow for the moon to impact the waves.'

'True. It's common knowledge now, but the Ainu would not have known, nor would they have the same concept of the devil that Japanese people or Westerners do. Only the word dusk has a commonality with our age.'

Dusk was growing at the same speed as our impatience. I suspected that, like a magic-eye poster or a riddle, all the pieces were there. All we needed to do was connect them in the right way to reveal the often painfully simple answer.

Yet the lake did not transform or terraform before our eyes, nor did any island erupt from it surface. An uneven glow spread across the water's surface as the sun descended, but apart from that there was no other indication of anything unusual about to occur.

Abruptly, Johnny sprinted down from the ledge to the lake, his rapid, uncontrolled pace verging on free-falling. At the lakeside in moments, he picked up a six-feet-long stick and, in a frenzy, started to randomly stab the water along the bank. He soon hollered in delight. His actions made me wonder if his fall from stress into madness was finally complete when suddenly, I had to question my own faculties: I saw Johnny walking on water, beating a path across the lake. At last, Chihiro and I began to understand the difference between fact and illusion. We started mapping the lake with our signal-dead mobile phone cameras, taking dozens of photographs from our vantage point. Knowing we only had moments to spare, we looked up to see Johnny a quarter of the way across the lake, pointing at a small opening into the mountain peak side. We went down to meet him and see if this miracle could be unravelled and explained.

We arrived at the lakeside just as Johnny returned, the water ankle deep where it should have submerged him completely. We walked into the water, and when we got to our knees, our descent stopped, then levelled out before slowly dipping to ankle level as we continued. The water heat was uncomfortable but not burning, and the sulphur fumes were weaker away from the lake's edge. I looked down into the water. It was black and devoid of any plant or animal life – not even basic algae.

'How is this even possible?' Chihiro gasped with glee.

'All I can think of is maybe the volcanic sediment has built up over the centuries, creating clear plates under the surface, which act like a false floor. You can feel them sway occasionally. I have heard of small islands appearing in the sea from volcanic eruptions, only to sink after a short time. Here, the calmness and containment of the lake may have let them slowly build up,' I surmised.

'That's why the sunlight gleaming off the lake is much brighter in some areas than others. It has less distance to travel and so noticeably glows more intently,' Johnny said, bowing to our silent applause.

We stood there debating, the majesty of this miracle already lost to us. It was as though we had just worked out a solution to the most impressive magic trick or illusion possible. The cave entrance, now faded back into the lake's bank, was barely visible, even though we were close. No wonder we missed it when we searched the lake before.

'We should collect our things and head for the cave. We only have one full day left to explore and find the rest of the statues before we start running low on food. The storm may still hit us, so we need to return to Japan as early as possible.'

Johnny was right, but neither Chihiro nor I tried to hide our uneasiness at his obviously insincere enthusiasm. We headed back to our rock overhang hotel to use the dying light to collect our things, then descend into our subterranean goal. Each of us had our own high-stake aims.

Chapter Forty-One

The sun was low, and the shadows were deep as we approached the lake's edge. The light was now so dim that we would have to make do with the photos Chihiro and I had taken on our phones of the reflective lake plates, hoping they were detailed enough to avoid falling into a sulphury dip. We all carried five-feet sticks to use as guide poles. Johnny and I brought all the equipment because Chihiro was still weak from seasickness and dehydration. She struggled even to move herself.

We had guessed that the cave entrance was no more than about 350 metres away in the mountainside from the lake's shoreline starting point, yet our course was not straight. The underwater mineral plates curved to the lake's sulphur vents, casting a ragged swirl to the pathway that narrowed and doubled back on itself numerous times. This made the walk twice as long as it needed to be. We went in single file, Johnny at the front, Chihiro in the middle, and me last.

Slowly and tentatively, we started edging across the lake in concentrated silence. We aimed to keep the path as central as possible, figuring the sediment plate would be thicker in the centre than the rim edges. The sediment plate rocked and jutted under our feet, our tapping sticks causing vibrations timed with our footsteps.

Soon, we were almost halfway to the cave, and with each footstep not leading to calamity, our confidence grew and our caution decreased. The single line turned to a wave, and our chatter rose as the entrance grew comfortably closer with each advancing step. The outline was smooth yet deep. I wondered if parts of the passageway would be underwater, a state not unknown in such situations.

I was contemplating our next step, how to navigate the passageway, without paying adequate attention to the present danger. One moment I was walking merrily on water Jesus Christ-style, the next, I was sinking like the Titanic, my head shrieking in pain, my limbs refusing to function, my backpack an anchor pulling me down. I remember the light dimming as I gasped for oxygen.

***

I awoke on the plate, spewing out water as my organs screamed for oxygen. Johnny was collapsed beside me, panting heavily after diving in to drag me from Davy Jones's grasp. Chihiro, stunned, watched as if this was all happening to another group of people, observing from afar as though uninvolved.

We lost the supplies I was carrying because Johnny had to disconnect and jettison them after the plate broke beneath me. Now we had less than one day of necessities left. Although I was still somewhat disoriented from recent events, we resumed our search. We went in as we reached the cave entrance, knowing we had no time to waste. My past thoughts about Johnny and Chihiro resurfaced: I wondered if I was most likely entering a cave with at least one murderer and two people, both of whom (in the short term, at least) had reasons to betray me. Johnny's might be to keep all the rewards for himself and have two fewer witnesses for the yakuza to deal with. Chihiro's reason might be the fear of knowing that one, if not both, of her Western cohorts had conspired to kill her mentor. Vengeance tinted by eternal academic glory might be almost impossible to resist, even for the noblest patron.

Chapter Forty-Two

There was no ledge in the passageway. The water was soon up to my neck as I doggy-paddled, still slightly woozy from my injuries. I knew there would be little time to fully recover with the little food and time we had left. Our head torches only lit the sides of the cave. When we faced forward, the black void swallowed their light beams. Still, we swam ahead until a ledge slowly emerged from the darkness. I clutched onto it, inhaling the surprisingly fresh air. I hoped there was another vent somewhere pointing to an easier path out. At last, we came inside the cave opening to dry land.

The cave was large enough to stand in, and I could easily reach the roof with an outstretched finger. The roof was cylinder shaped and led into darkness. The sides had been smoothed down to a shine by eons of dripping water. A breeze of cool air came in blasts, probably from the wind. We began inspecting the walls, looking for any markings that might be man-made. Chihiro asked Johnny for the camera he was carrying and began photographing the pool we had emerged from and our landing spot to document each inch of the entrance. Then she walked into the darkness, leaving Johnny and me to follow.

For a moment, I thought the path was flanked with eerily regular rows of stalagmites haphazardly staggered upwards until my eyes adjusted to the gloom. Then I realised they were not limestone pillars spun by millenniums of water drips. They sat in parallel pairs on a bright white, glowing, thick base cylinder that shrank with height to a pointed tip. I realised why the pillars seemed vaguely familiar: I had been carrying the same carved material for months! I gazed, awestruck, at the woolly mammoth tusk pillars at least 4,000 years old. They were there before the pharaohs expelled the Jews from Egypt, before Helen fled with Paris from Troy.

It was now clear we were going deeper into the mountainside, the passageway in front of us having a slight downward slope. There were occasional shallow puddles, the odd small fish skeletons and rotten foliage sludge. I was busy studying the floor when gasps from Chihiro and Johnny snapped my attention back to them.

It was an entrance into a large chamber, but the opening was not what had made my companions swoon; the stone archway at the doorway had caught their attention. It was embedded with symbols and figures carved out of the cave wall in the same style as my statue. A sun surrounded by five rays rested at the arch's peak. A carved panel representing each of the locations and trials we were on to reach our goal ran down the left side. The panel began with the mountain peak of Mount Rausu. The next was the Shoji Valley, with its creeping river. Then the stone circle we discovered at Natsuki Mekko beach leading us across the sea to the lake. Finally, the lake with the pathway etched across leading to the cave entrance. The carvings were framed with smaller tusks. Fine lines identified each animal sacrifice undertaken to make the arch. Long, thin walrus tusks sat next to a short squat tooth of a sabre-toothed cat. Their scratch-drawn bodies were wrapped around the panel, the walrus caught in mid-dive, the sabre-toothed cat in a half-pounce.

'We made it after all.' Johnny sighed, his tone heavy with relief.

They studied the archway while Chihiro passed me my Ainu book before frantically clicking her camera. Slowly, Johnny ran his fingers up and down the arch's spines. I flashed my torchlight into the archway-framed chamber, which showed itself as a large cave. My light beam didn't reach the far wall, so I swept it across the floor, pushing across a barrage of strange scurrying shadows. I walked through the archway into the chamber.

At first, I thought the shadows were rows of small boulders randomly placed, all roughly round. Yet there was something instinctively unsettling there. I walked towards the nearest object to find it covered in a thick layer of dirt. The next two were the same, the only difference being that some were egg-shaped and others half-covered domes. They were spread across the whole floor of the chamber. I temporarily lost interest as I flashed my torch to the back of the chamber. I decided to take a closer look.

As I walked closer, the torchlight refracted brightly as though it was the room's private sun, its yellow ribbons of light cutting the gloom. The glint of gold was undeniable; the question was how much it was worth. I saw what looked to be piles of oval gold coins called Koban – the main currency of the Tokugawa Shogunate from 1601 to about 1867, when it was phased out under the Meiji Restoration. The coins were nestled with Buddha statues happily smiling next to roaring, emerald-eyed jade dragons. I was so mesmerised, I tripped on one of the stones I had forgotten about. I tumbled down.

I stayed there, dazed. I could hear the footsteps of Chihiro and Johnny behind me, having finally broken free of the arch's trance. When they entered, gasps echoed round the chamber. I turned to see the stone I had tripped over was broken like an eggshell. My hand had smashed another trying to break my fall. The one in the front, the one I had barely missed, stared back with hollowed eye sockets, its jaw lying twisted on the floor.

They were human skulls, hundreds of them, all long decayed and coated in dirt. Now I could see their features protruding through the grime – a casual nose point, a single, soiled eye socket. Others were encased in layers of mud, each one indistinguishable from the next. They were all buried at different levels. Some had shoulders poking out; for others, only the crowns of their heads were visible.

'*Hitogaki*!' Chihiro gasped, her first genuine show of emotion in days.

'English, please,' Johnny politely asked.

'It's a human hedge. It was a form of Japanese human sacrifice in ancient times when servants were buried up to their neck around their master's grave to cry and grieve for him till they died of starvation or were eaten by wild animals. It was finally put to an end in the sixth century, yet rumours persist that the practice was carried on for much longer.'

'Looks like for once the rumours were right,' I murmured, brushing bits of skull from my hand and shaking fragments off my boot.

The clanging of metal-on-metal echoed behind us. I turned to see Johnny running piles of coins between his fingers, flickering like a metallic waterfall. Using all three torch beams, Chihiro went to join him to investigate the wooden altar made of a large carved bowl. It held the treasure, which sat on a steep wooden cone about two metres high and fifteen centimetres wide. Its contents flashed back many unashamed golden smiles. Sunlight streamed from a shaft cut into the ceiling onto the altar, revealing a gallery of precious stones and cut jewels kaleidoscopically winking back. Hilts of samurai swords protruding from the hoard added a touch of elegance. I would have investigated further, but now another form emerged from the retreating shadows.

It was a second altar with a stone base on three large circle steps, each about five metres high, rising like a staggered pyramid as opposed to the bowl crowned altar that had captured Johnny and Chihiro's attention so completely about 4.5 metres away. There were no gold coins or jewels, just a number of tusk animal statues – the same family as the one in my bag, all beautiful in their own way. There must have been over twenty *kamuy* statues, about half on the altar and the rest scatted on the steps. A few were half-buried in the mud. I could identify some of the more popular ones, such as Kim-un-amuy, the Bear God. It had a different texture and shine than my own statue, so it was possibly made of bear bone or a large tooth or claw. There was Cikap-kamuy, the God of Owls, made almost seamlessly from multiple pieces of owl bones, one for each limb and wing. I also found Hoyau, the Dragon God, cut out of what looked like a rib bone so large and dense I suspected it was Jurassic in origin. Using my Ainu book, I managed to match many more *kamuy* to their carved idols, from majestic animals carved out of various sizes and bones to grotesque human statues of demons and deities, all cut of the same material and in keeping with the possible theme of human bones.

'Look, Chihiro, Johnny, I've found the other statues.'

Neither cared, as both seemed to have been struck down by gold sickness. Chihiro was trying on jewels with one hand while photographing with the other. Johnny was admiring coins, then picked up a Buddha statue, possibly of solid gold, the emerald eyes mockingly waving back at him. Actually, the statue was quite dented and gaudy. For Johnny, it would seem gaudy gold won over majestic carved ivory. But now, their problems centred around whether Chihiro could have her historical artefacts, thus find personal glory, and Johnny would have the money to pay back the yakuza, thus find personal preservation where settled. I was only interested in the true goal of the journey. Now, they began to act increasingly like children, drawing and wildly swinging samurai swords at each other, oblivious to the danger of accidental disembowelment or decapitation.

The beam of sunlight was very low, just managing to illuminate the whole cave. The altars stood in stark contrast: one's glitter and glow increased, the other sank into the shadows as the audience of the dead silently watched. In the shadowy light, I could now see the whole floor and noticed there were no heads around my stone base altar. Yet at Johnny and Chihiro's altar, they were densely packed, almost on top of each other. What's more, they all faced the same way: towards the entrance. There were even a few stragglers before the arch.

Suddenly, I heard barely audible running water echoing around the room's edge. It proliferated in pace and noise by the moment.

'Quiet!' I called out to all in vain, but they weren't paying attention. My presence had been forgotten in their greedy hope of future acclaim and wealth.

The sunlight beam was growing in strength, now on the verge of crossing the middle point of the room. The water noise was steadily growing.

'"All life is caught between the devil and the dusk",' I repeated so softy it was barely a murmur.

As my eyes adjusted to the thin sunlight, I noticed that a rag on one of the skulls looked like a half-rotten baseball cap. As Johnny and Chihiro continued their childish shenanigans, the puzzle pieces fell into place for me in a dozen heartbeats. Unfortunately, that was a half-dozen too long.

Chihiro turned and stepped towards me and suddenly began to sink to her knees. Johnny pointed and laughed at her as the mud floor devoured his own ankles. Annoyed, they struggled for a few moments till they realised the mud was eating them alive. Their growing panic and thrashing only hastened their plunge. They leapt up to climb onto the wooden altar base, but this, too, was being consumed by the rising mud, and their fingers slipped off. The mud crept up to the first stone step of my stone step altar, then flowed over it.

A minute was all there was to it. If a minute earlier we had all stood on the stone step altar, we all would have been saved. Those now on the wooden altar – Chihiro and Johnny – were damned.

'My feet are on the bottom. I may be able to get to you!' Johnny shouted to me. But from my vantage point on the stone step altar, it was clear he was making no progress, just churning up his captor. The mud had now taken Chihiro to her throat. Her fingertips poked out helplessly, and it seemed that she, too, had found the floor.

'All we need to do is wait for the mud to dry and harden. Then you can dig us out,' Chihiro screamed on the verge of hysterics.

I think we all suspected that what was happening was no coincidence, but like all tragedies played out in front of you, it was easier to hope for the best and not to acknowledge the facts. A rumbling silenced me before I could reply.

Water poured through holes in the walls, spewing in at high pressure. In moments, a shallow layer of water appeared on the mud's surface. Whether manufactured, natural, or a mixture of both, the chamber was a death trap that flooded every day in the evening. A watermark level just below the last stone step on my altar was a testament to its consistency.

From my pedestal on the stone step altar, I could not help them without meeting the same fate. Any hope of the mud losing its grip via dilution by the gushing water seemed unlikely as the water sat on top as through the mud was clay.

'You've got to help me! Help us!'

'How?' I asked with aghast hopelessness.

I swear, even in the gloom, I saw the light in their eyes dim slightly. The water was now at Chihiro's lips. It began to spill in, causing her to spit out between gasps. Johnny was flailing, his struggle weakening him. They now knew that short of divine intervention, they were doomed to die. I was powerless to help, and any anger they may have had towards my good fortune to be in the right place at the right time was replaced with self-pity over all they could have been, soon to be lost without drama or applause.

Chihiro was underwater now, and Johnny could do nothing but stare on in horror. His own fate was being played out before his eyes like a macabre live performance. Her head flicked violently side to side, anything to loosen the mud for another brief sip of air to buy a few more moments of life. Desperation racked her face with each attempt. In one final try, she managed to get one breath through the tip of her nose. Worn out now, knowing defeat was inevitable, she calmly submerged into the water and mud, holding her breath before one, last, violent jolt freed her from life.

The water was now lapping midway up Johnny's chin. His eyes fixed on Chihiro's underwater corpse before breaking out of his trance for one final, desperate, volley of energy to escape his fate. For every inch he managed to pull himself up, the moment he rested, he sunk another two further into the mud. His hopelessness grew with every try. He started to slap the water away, using his arms as a scoop. With the water now brushing his bottom lip, I could see he was exhausted. Fear of the inevitable seeped into his face.

'Mike, please, please, Mike, ple—'

That was his last minute testament on Earth. No last moment reprieve, no chaotic miracle to save him. I wondered if, maybe for the first time in his life, Johnny had fully faced the consequences of his actions. His thrashing head had kicked up enough mud to cover his face and save me from having to watch his death grimace. By the time the mud cloud dissipated, he was long gone. Everything he was, everything he could have been, had been taken in a game he never knew he had entered. Losing a bet he never knew, his life's promise was diluted into the water.

Chapter Forty-Three

Now there was nothing left for me to do but wait. My two companions glared at me with dead-eyed accusations, their heads poking out of the mud like their countless unnamed companions. The water was rising steadily. Judging by the watermark on the walls, there would be enough room for air in the passageway we used to enter the cave. If I had to swim the length in one breath, I suspected my fate would be the same as my recently departed friends.

The water eased to a trickle, just spilling over on to the top stone step of my altar. The sun's light beam was now shining on the archway entrance to the room. The water was only about six feet deep. I stretched my legs and rotated my arms as cramps were the last thing I wanted to happen. Being felled by a simple muscle spasm midswim would be almost comical after surviving so much. I had not had food or drink in hours, and the rest of the supplies were buried with Johnny, now sodden and ruined. I would only get one chance and in fading light. I set off.

As I slowly swam over Chihiro and Johnny's corpses, I tried not to look, but the temptation was too great. It almost felt like a macabre duty. Their lips where blue, their eyes were placid.

As I passed over them, the waves shifted their hair. Small fish that had come in with the rising water were inspecting the new flesh ornaments, making tours into ears and scream-stretched mouths before swimming away, all interest soon lost.

I swam through the arch to find the slowly filling tunnel with only just enough room to grab a breath between strokes. I made sure my head torch was secure, filled my lungs with three deep breaths, and pushed off. The jagged rocks I had easily avoided on the walk in now snagged my clothes and ripped my muscles like large piranha teeth, and I felt a searing burning. I bashed my head against the side every few feet as I rose to gasp for air, leaving me punch drunk by the time I saw the light at the end of the tunnel. The literal light! I just had enough energy and coordination to pull my bloodied self onto the sediment plate ledge on the lake.

I lay there panting, all my limbs stinging and on the verge of cramping. The sun had almost set, the air was already cooling, and without the sunlight, the sediment plate had already disappeared into the water's darkness. I crawled back across the lake on the sediment plates to the shore land, double-checking and feeling out every movement before fully committing. I knew that if I fell in, I would not have the energy to drag myself out and would finally suffer the same fate as my former companions after avoiding it earlier.

An hour later, I made it to dry land. The night had settled, its cold wind increasing the deep aching in my overly used muscles. I stood and stretched, then slowly and shakily headed back to the rock overhang. I prayed that the few supplies left there had not been stolen by any overly inquisitive wildlife. Now out of imminent danger, my hunger taunted me with grumbling and whining. I sat on the rock eating one of the few remaining energy bars and watching the lights of Rausu flickering across the sea in the distance.

Only now did I have the time to examine my battered and bruised body with bloody, snagged limbs and torn skin. Still, these were inconsequential compared to the mental wounds, leaving deep scars I doubted would ever truly heal. Now out of relative danger, I could start to come to terms with what I had witnessed and the actions I would have to take.

Epilogue

One month later

After barely escaping a watery abyss, I was immediately plunged into a different breed of nightmare, but before I tell you where I am now, I need to finish the story that put me here.

Once I found the rock overhang, I retrieved the compass, money, food and a small bag with my few remaining clothes we had left there. Then I rested fitfully for the night, hoping the ghosts of Johnny and Chihiro would not visit me Dickens-style. The next day, it took till late afternoon to sneak back to where we had hidden the boat. Our makeshift camouflage was almost too effective, causing me to walk past the collage of leaves and twigs twice, panic growing with each step. After a few hours of restless sleep, I rowed back to Rausu. Thankfully, I avoided lousy weather and other unnecessary dramas and landed at a beach just out of town.

As I made my way back to Tokyo by bus, then train, the same plaguing nightmares about Johnny and Chihiro robbed me of rest and reprise. I knew that only upon my return to Tokyo would I have to begin coming to terms with what I had witnessed and weigh the decisions I would have to make. If I sent an anonymous tip about the cave to the Russians without evidence, it was highly unlikely they would take it seriously, even though they owned the island and would benefit from the financial gain and historical legacy of that find. While Johnny and Chihiro had shattered my trust by their actions, I felt bad simply abandoning them. Still, I could hardly pull their corpses out of the cave by myself, especially since a month had passed and who knows what state they would be in. Then there was the fact I was wanted in connection with Professor Haruto's murder, not to mention by one of the most powerful organised crime syndicates in the world. They would be looking for me, and with my passport gone and limited funds, my options were low.

I headed south to Tokyo, scanning one of the half-dozen newspapers at Shinjuku Station for any photo of me. Finding one staring back at me meant I was now officially on the run. I was relieved that the photo, a security camera still, was blurred. My long hair had hidden my features right when the camera caught me. The only other photograph of me had been taken at the immigration booth on my arrival in Japan about a year ago. That photo showed a different man – his face was framed with tightly pulled-back hair, distorted by twelve hours of confined sleepless travel and in full view. Only the most dedicated searcher would have a chance of identifying me. I decided to travel to Osaka, the largest of Japan's southern cities, hoping I would finally find a moment of rest there. Here, interest in the story of the professor's murder had waned, but I still felt the need for caution. Unfortunately, in Sapporo, the story still blazed. Every internet local news site refused to let the story die in peace.

As for my lost passport, there was little I could do, in reality, without risking being arrested by authorities who would have been alerted. I could go to the British embassy to plead my case, but who would believe such a tale? And even if they did, the first question would be why I hadn't come forward sooner. I doubt the excuse of being swept up in such implausible events would suffice or that they would have any sympathy for a man in his early twenties acting so irresponsibly regarding an adventure that was, for all purposes, an illegal treasure hunt replete with gangsters, betrayal and murder. There was no way for me to leave the country as I would need a counterfeit passport, which could only be obtained through the yakuza, who were undoubtedly hunting me, very unhappy at how their prize investment had turned out. So I decided against even trying to attempt that option, as even making a vague enquiry would be a modern-day kamikaze mission for me.

I found an internet café in Osaka's Kamagasaki district, Japan's poorest district. I emailed Japanese and Russian media outlets detailing the incredible events leading to our discovery of the lake and its secret cave on Kunashir Island. I described the ancient treasures and artefacts we found, the skeletons, and the horrific deaths of Johnny and Chihiro. I also revealed the yakuza's alarming threats on Johnny's life, hoping the police would get to them.

A mere two days later, I found a hiding place in the Ninja and Geisha Capsule Hotel, a name revealing the creative imagination limits of its owner. The hotel's floor-to-ceiling wooden panels harshly radiated with neon lights as soulless as a bleak funeral parlour. The capsules were little more than two-story shelves, barely containing a bed and a television on the ceiling. Their décor had as much appeal as a cheap, oversized coffin. Ensconced in my capsule, I was falling asleep watching TV when breaking news about the fateful lake that had dramatically changed my life a mere month earlier interrupted the programme. Formerly unknown to the world, the lake was now centre stage. I jerked awake, all ears. But the news anchors were babbling enthusiastically in Japanese, hiding the details from me as decisively as the cave's whereabouts had been hidden from us. I had to wait for the English translation in the next day's newspaper to discover the full story. So I turned out the lights and fell into a restless sleep.

***

A month later, I woke up feeling like I was swimming through the passageway again, gasping for air as I did most nights. I sat up, rubbed my eyes open and shook the bad dream out of my head. Then I pulled on some rumpled clothes and went out to find a paper with the ongoing story. It was big news, easy to find, and it was definitely a mind-blower. Clearly, a whole lot of people had done a lot of work to bring this story to life.

The article claimed that at least one hundred bodies had been found in the cave in various states of decay; all those from every corner of Japan unfortunate enough to have been enticed by a statue and manuscript. Preliminary carbon dating showed that the victims' ages were spread over two centuries. A few of the oldest bodies dated back to the decade after the Tokugawa Treasure theft. Two missing persons from the mid-1970s were the most recent before Johnny and Chihiro. The clay mud had preserved faces twisted in horror at their moments of death. Apparently, the gold and silver of the Tokugawa Treasure found on the wooden altar was a mere fraction of the originally stolen hoard.

Another month went by till more details emerged. Ultrasound scans of the cave floor looking for more deeply buried bodies found channels cut deep into the rock to aid water flow. The Ainu had mixed the area with a layer of sand and a base of stones to ensure that it drained every day after flooding, a composition which, within twelve hours, would harden enough to walk on easily. The Ainu had taken a harmless natural feature and, with a few tweaks, weaponised it to almost one hundred per cent lethality. I suspect I'm the trap's sole survivor. Academic circles raged over the motive for creating such an effective and devastatingly cruel water guillotine trap, which revealed how genius can reside in the simplest form. The growing consensus was that revenge – the oldest and most soulless of man's primal instincts – was the motive. The Ainu people's last meaningful act of defiance against the Meiji Restoration was ambushing the convoy carrying their bone statues and the Tokugawa Treasure. But this put them in an ironic predicament.

On the one hand, they had obtained enough immense wealth to support the next one hundred generations in opulent luxury. On the other, spending more than the minimum amount risked alerting Meiji Restoration agents and bringing their full force of murderous fury into the lives of the Ainu people. The Ainu had no choice but to hide the treasure. Yet after having a little taste of revenge, their appetite seemed to have become unquenchable. Without the resources to wage a conventional resistance to the Meiji Restoration, they had to create a more novel method. So the Ainu used the bone statues and poems as lures and bait, knowing that greed for the gold and jewels would overwhelm and blind (at least momentarily) most people, even those with the purest intentions. In this way, they created the cave's water guillotine trap. The legion of interloping skeletons was a testament to its efficiency.

It is now believed that the Ainu placed the statues throughout Japan at a rate of a few each decade from the 1890s to the 1960s, when the Japanese authorities finally extinguished the last few remnants of the Ainu culture. Japanese kanji completely replaced Ainu kanji around the turn of the century. After the Ainu finally mastered it, the riddle in Japanese kanji was always the same, letter for letter. The parchment was often found entombed with the random victims chosen by ill luck to find the statues, leading them to be sacrificed by their own simple curiosity. My statue must have been one of the originals meant for those who had captured its owner in Inaka just before he burned their village to the ground on the Modoro cape. I found it over a century later while diving. My statue was to be found after his death, leading them to their deaths and his revenge. Ironically, the fire was far more effective and thorough.

From my email description, the yakuza, who had harassed and blackmailed Johnny, were soon found and arrested at their pachinko parlour address. I noted how a trial will be held "at a later date" and the charges against them "will soon be disclosed" – such is the clandestine nature of the Japanese criminal justice system. Since the "evidence" I shared in my email was all circumstantial, I suspect the police have found other compelling physical evidence against them. Indeed, the trial may have a judge who decides their fate, not a jury. The good news is this will halt their pursuit of me – at least for the time being. Still, the yakuza have deep pockets and wide influence, so I doubt I will ever be truly off the hook.

So who stole my passport? And who murdered the professor? As for the professor, a partial fingerprint was found on one of the professor's statues, the most probable murder weapon pointing straight to the culprit, but the investigation is still ongoing. Who the print belongs to has yet to be released publicly. It has been rumoured that there were residual traces of Rohypnol in one of the corpses of my two former friends, meaning I and one other were drugged the night of the professor's slaying. A twist in the murder investigation is that two of the three prime suspects are now themselves deceased in the most bizarre of circumstances. Thus, my absence must have raised the investigation's stress level from a mild headache to a massive migraine.

If I had to guess, I would say it was Johnny who murdered the professor. He had the motive to keep the treasure to himself to buy a way out the hole he had dug himself. As it was the yakuza who gave him the shovel in the first place, he may have just been prolonging the inevitable. Yet Johnny was foreign and hardy inconspicuous. He would have looked very out of place at night in the suburbs, and so far, no witnesses have come forward. As for Chihiro, I don't see how murder was necessary for her goals. External glory, after all, is often prized above temporal gold in academic circles. Still, there was a coldness and determination to her nature, meaning she may have viewed murder as a way to keep all the glory for herself. Either way, whoever it was would have to kill the other two to guarantee their silence, so from my perspective, if they had lived, it was a one hundred per cent losing phenomenon.

Who stole my passport? Perhaps it was Johnny to keep me in Japan as I was his only link to Chihiro. Yet the same logic says it could have been Chihiro to ensure she was not left at Johnny's mercy. I guess now I will never know.

As for Johnny and Chihiro, their deaths have been declared as having technically drowned by their own folly – not by failing to unwrap the poem's final metaphor, the real reason, if you ask me. The treasure was found on Russian territory, although that has been disputed since World War II. So it will be the diplomats who dictate the course of what I suspect will be a painfully slow resolution process.

PATRICK IRELAND

***

There is no official term for what I am now; some call it *Jouhatsu*, others *Yongie*. The rough English translation is "evaporated people" – those with no documentation or set address who drift between the realms of legality and necessity, not wholly legal or trustworthy but needed in society to fill in the gaps in the insecure work and repulsive professions. Although ignored, whole systems would collapse in just one day without them. So now I wait, my life stuck in limbo, reliving the drowning of Johnny and Chihiro in nightly nightmares.

I have done my best to change my appearance to avoid detection, cutting my long hair short and growing a thin beard. I now look slightly ridiculous. Believe me, such things are nowhere near as easy or as effective as in the movies. I exist doing odd jobs. Some are bizarre, like pretending to be a catholic priest complete with cassock and clerical collar for wedding photographs. Mostly, I teach English to the outcasts of the *Burakumin* class, a group comprised of the least noble of professions such as butchers, slaughterhouse workers and undertakers. It is a historic caste of untouchables in Japanese society, still living in small ghettos scattered in all major cities. A millennium of discrimination weighs them down, like the nearly invisible Korean community who lives ignored in history's shadow.

So now I wait.

I live in cash-only apartments where no questions are asked, no ID is needed or name registered. In these places, everyone drifts by like ghosts in corridors and stairwells with as little acknowledgement as possible and only enough awareness to avoid colliding into each other. Our life paths are disjointed, fragile and so light as to be almost transparent. We can leave at a moment's notice to disappear into the void of over 120 million people. An irony in my situation is that my name is now synonymous with histories of other famous adventurers. Almost purely by accident, my name is spoken in the same breath as Howard Carter's discovery of the Tutankhamun tomb and Franklin's lost Arctic expedition to find the northwest passage. What's my discovery? It is now known the world over as the Tokugawa Treasure and Ainu Trove. A new industry appeared almost overnight for those foolish enough to spend their life hunting for myths by running around the Shiretoko Peninsula and sneaking onto Kunashir Island – to the great annoyance of the Russians.

As for "the devil and the dusk", well, it turns out the devil is nothing more than being powerless; whether watching people rapidly drown or die slowly from cancer, it makes no difference. There is no justice in the world, just an unleased fury of helplessness after ignoring the small telltale signs.

So now I wait.

I wait for a knock by the police or immigration services. The best-case scenario is for a breakthrough in the murder case that can prove my innocence, let me tell my side of the story, and finally come out the cold shadows of the legion of the lost.

But till then, there still two months of summer to experience. I have clients to see, and English won't teach itself. In a country as vast as Japan, the past needs a quick step and large stride to catch you. At dodging life's trials, I have to give myself an A.

So now I wait.